The sun ha⟨...⟩ warm light was radiating through the barn

"Funny," Clint said softly. "I could have sworn you wanted me to kiss you earlier."

Samantha lifted her chin.

Back off, he told himself. But he couldn't stop. She was like a newborn foal—skittish and standoffish, but something he was tempted to tame.

"*You* wanted to kiss *me*," she corrected.

"You know," he said, giving in to the urge to touch her, his fingers making contact with the side of her neck, "I think you're right."

He just meant to give her a little peck on the lips. But the moment he tasted her, the moment his lips made contact with her own, he was lost.

Dear Reader,

I've always been horse crazy. When I was a little girl I would beg my parents every year to buy me a horse for Christmas. I think they hoped my fascination with all things equine would eventually go away because they ignored my requests until I was thirteen years old. They probably grew tired of listening to my pleas because they eventually gave in.

Guess what? Thirty years later, I'm still just as nuts about my four-legged friends as I was when I was a child. So when someone suggested I write a romance novel about the animals I love I felt like a complete doofus. Why hadn't I thought of that before?

The result of that suggestion, *The Wrangler,* was a labor of love. It was truly a joy to write about the animals that mean so much to me. I can honestly say that the soft nicker of a horse has lifted my spirits more times than I can count. My own American quarter horse, Bippity Boppin' Along (aka Bippy) has gotten me through some of the toughest times of my life.

I hope you enjoy *The Wrangler.* Whether you're a horse lover or not, it's my sincerest wish to always…*always* bring you tales that make you laugh and cry.

Pamela Britton

P.S. If you're interested in reading more about me *or* my horses, please visit my Web site at www.pamelabritton.com.

The Wrangler
PAMELA BRITTON

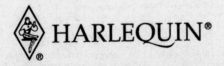

TORONTO • NEW YORK • LONDON
AMSTERDAM • PARIS • SYDNEY • HAMBURG
STOCKHOLM • ATHENS • TOKYO • MILAN • MADRID
PRAGUE • WARSAW • BUDAPEST • AUCKLAND

Recycling programs
for this product may
not exist in your area.

ISBN-13: 978-0-373-75289-8

THE WRANGLER

Copyright © 2009 by Pamela Britton.

www.eHarlequin.com

Printed in U.S.A.

ABOUT THE AUTHOR

With over a million books in print, Pamela Britton likes to call herself the best-known author nobody's ever heard of. Of course, that's begun to change thanks to a certain licensing agreement with that little racing organization known as NASCAR. Nowadays it's not unusual to hear her books being discussed by the likes of Jay Leno, Keith Olbermann or Stephen Colbert. Flip open a magazine and you might read about her, too, in *Sports Illustrated*, *Entertainment Weekly* or Southwest Airlines' *Spirit Magazine*. Channel surf and you might see her on *The Today Show*, *Nightline* or *World News*.

But before the glitz and glamour of NASCAR, Pamela wrote books that were frequently voted the best of the best by the *Detroit Free Press*, Barnes & Noble (two years in a row) and *RT Book Reviews* magazine. She's won numerous writing awards, including the National Readers' Choice, and has been nominated for Romance Writers of America's Golden Heart.

When not following the race circuit, Pamela writes full-time from her ranch in northern California, where she lives with her husband, daughter and, at last count, twenty-one four-legged friends.

Books by Pamela Britton

HARLEQUIN AMERICAN ROMANCE

 985—COWBOY LESSONS
1040—COWBOY TROUBLE
1122—COWBOY M.D.
1143—COWBOY VET
1166—COWGIRL'S CEO

HQN BOOKS

DANGEROUS CURVES
IN THE GROOVE
ON THE EDGE
TO THE LIMIT
TOTAL CONTROL
ON THE MOVE

Chapter One

He was six-foot-one of rock-hard muscle. Every last inch of him one hundred percent, prime-cut cowboy.

And he caused Samantha Davies to slam on the brakes.

Clinton McAlister, she thought, lifting her foot and slowly edging over to the side of the road. It had to be.

He pounded a metal post into the ground to her right, oblivious to her arrival at the Baer Mountain Ranch. She'd been told what he looked like by a couple of the local townspeople, right down to the distinctive brown and white feather tucked into the cowboy hat he wore. What she hadn't expected, no, what no verbal description could ever convey, was the sheer size of him. The way his sleeveless white shirt clung to his sweat-stained body. How his muscular arms glistened beneath a noonday sun.

"My, my, my," she murmured.

Okay. Get a grip.

She wasn't here to ogle him. She had a business proposition for Mr. McAlister, and there was no time like the present.

She checked her rearview mirror. No one behind her. Not that she'd expected anyone this far from civilization. She was on a private gravel road, with nothing but acres and acres of Montana grassland stretching to the left and right. Straight ahead, the Big Belt Mountain range stood, snow covering the tops of them like icing on a cake. They seemed to be far off in the distance, but she knew the Baer family owned land right up into those mountains. The sheer scope of their property took her breath away.

Even from inside her road-weary car she could hear the clink-clink-clink of metal-on-metal. It must have masked the sound of her approach because the cowboy still hadn't turned.

She shut off her car, thought for a second about honking, then nixed the idea. Better to greet him personally.

A stiff breeze all but slapped her in the face the instant she stepped out of the car's warm interior. There was a thunderstorm off to her left. Though her vision wasn't what it used to be, she'd been able to follow its progress as she'd driven. The wind was pressing Mr. McAlister's buttoned-down shirt against his back, and tugging at her own short brown strands.

"Hello," she called out.

He still didn't hear her. The breeze had snatched her words away. That same wind almost caught Mr. McAlister's hat. He reached for it quickly, and had to turn toward her, dipping his head into the wind to stop it from blowing away.

He caught sight of her.

"Hi," she said, waving.

He didn't answer. But that was okay. Sam was incapable of speech, anyway. His shirt was open in the front. And that chest…

Oh, my.

Six perfectly symmetrical muscles bulged, the upper

portion covered by a light dusting of hair. But even more startling were his eyes. Luminous, they were. Blue. But so light in color, they almost seemed to glow. Those eyes narrowed in on her.

"Sorry to interrupt," she said.

His blond eyebrows drew together in what could only be called a frown. Obviously, he hadn't been expecting company. Not surprising given they were at least thirty miles from Williams, Montana—and at least two miles from his home—if her navigation system was correct. She must have been a sight standing there in her fancy floral skirt, white blouse and sensible shoes.

She should have worn jeans.

"Can I help you?" he called out at last. She hadn't gone blind just yet—not officially, at least—but she didn't need eyes to know he was *not* happy to see her. Why? she wondered.

"Do you always treat your fence posts like that?" she asked, trying to coax a smile out of him. "Or was it something it said?"

He glanced at the dark green rod he'd been pounding into the ground. On either side of it strands of barbwire hung like Christmas tinsel, glinting in the sun.

"Someone ran into the old one," he said, nodding toward an L-shaped post on the ground. "Needs to be replaced before our cattle get loose."

He delivered the words in a monotone. No hint of emotion. Not even a tiny twinkle in his eyes.

"Does that happen often?" she asked with a grin of her own. "Cows making a run for the hills?"

He tipped his hat back, wiped his forehead with his arm while he scanned her blue rental car. He wore gloves, she noticed, the beige leather palms worn smooth like black patent leather.

"More often than you might think," he said.

"Oh, yeah?" she asked. "Then it must be true."

He stared at her. "What must be true?"

"That the grass is always greener on the other side." She amped up the volume of her smile. "Or taller, as the case may be."

"If you've lost your way," he said after a long moment, "the main road is back the other direction." He lifted the metal pole he'd been using to pound the post into the ground.

"Actually," she persisted, making her way around the front of her car, "I'm here to see *you*."

He straightened again.

"At least, I *think* I'm here to see you." Her rubber soles crunched, eating up the rocks, with every step she took. "You *are* Clinton McAlister, aren't you?"

But she knew he was and if she thought he'd appeared irritated before, it was nothing compared to the glance he shot her now. "Look, lady. Whatever you're selling, I ain't buying. So you can just turn that car right around. I'm not interested."

"I'm not selling anything."

His eyebrows lifted. "No?"

This was the man who'd graduated from University of California Davis magna cum laude, who had a degree in veterinary medicine? Who used words like *ain't* and *lady*…like some kind of cartoon cowboy?

She'd been told what to expect. Sort of. Because what people had failed to tell her was how incredibly handsome he was. Sam was tall, well above average height, and so she wasn't used to men who stood a full head taller than herself. And he was fit. She'd always been attracted to men with wide shoulders, but Clinton McAlister looked more like a member of a rowing team than a cowboy.

The storm in the distance let out a rumble, one that sounded close by. They both turned. Rain hung in streamers from the bottom of a nearby cloud, the top so bibulous it resembled some sort of gigantic tick. Samantha began to wonder if they shouldn't seek cover.

"I'm here to talk to you about the Baer Mountain Mustangs," she said, over the fading sound of thunder.

That got his attention. She could see his pupils flare with something, although what exactly that emotion was she couldn't tell.

"Don't have any idea what you're talking about," he said, turning back to his task.

She rushed forward. "Mr. McAlister, wait," she said. "I know you're thinking I'll just go away if you deny it, but I won't. I'm not like the people who wrote books and articles on your horses. The ones you managed to send away without confirming that the Baer Mountain Mustangs live on your property. But I *know* they're here—the herd of horses whose roots trace back to the Native Americans who settled this land. I've heard first-hand from one of your former wranglers."

There was an embankment to the right of the road, one whose steep slope was camouflaged by thick grass. Unfortunately, with her narrowing field of vision, she neglected to calculate just how sharp an incline it was. She went careening toward him like a wind-driven beach ball, very nearly skidding into him. The only reason she didn't was because he reached out and stopped her. Samantha gasped.

He was sweaty. His body was hard. He smelled like leather and sage.

And she was very, *very* attracted to him.

"Lady, get in your car and drive back to town. I don't know nothing about Baer Mountain Mustangs and that storm's coming fast. Road'll be washed out if you don't hurry."

She finally caught her breath, stepped back from him. "Sorry," she said, dusting off her lap—though she hadn't gotten her skirt dirty. "About almost knocking you over, but I'm not going anywhere. Not until I see them."

He was back to glaring at her again and Samantha couldn't help staring at his eyes. They were the most remarkable color she'd ever seen and it was all she could do not to lean in and examine them closer. So blue. So light. So…pure.

"You're wasting your time," he said, turning away from her.

She was almost relieved that he'd broken eye contact. "Wasting my time how?" she asked. "In getting you to admit they exist?"

He picked up the metal tool again—he'd dropped it to stop her awkward descent—and she noticed then that it was a large pipe that was capped off at one end. He fit it over the top of the fence post and then, with a bunching of muscles, he lifted, shoving the pipe down hard.

Bam.

"Ouch," she cried, plugging her ears. It was like being inside a bell.

Clinton McAlister didn't appear to notice.

She moved away from him. Her peripheral vision might be fading fast, but a sudden darkening of the ground around them told her that the thunderstorm was almost on top of them—just as he'd predicted.

Bam.

"Mr. McAlister," she said during a break in sound, "I know that, somehow, the Baer family has managed to hide the mustangs all these years." She covered her ears again just in time to avoid the next bang. "And I know you're the man in charge of the secret herd."

He faced her. Sam let loose a sigh of relief. "Time for you to go," was all he said. He pointed behind her.

Sam turned. The thunderstorm. It was close enough that she could smell rain in the air.

"If I were you, I'd get under cover fast," he said, reaching in his pocket. He pulled out a metallic rod of some sort. Sam watched as he made quick work of attaching the loose wire to the metal post.

"Just how'd you get out here, anyway?" she asked.

The smile he gave her could only be called smug. He whistled.

Almost instantly she heard the sound of hooves, and if there was one thing she knew, it was horseflesh. The animal that cantered toward her was one of the most beautiful dappled grays she'd ever seen. Black mane and tail, black legs, and a pair of eyes nearly as luminous as his owner's.

A Baer Mountain Mustang. She would bet her life on it.

The gelding—or was it a stallion?—came to a sliding stop practically right next to them, Clinton shooting her a glance—as if curious to see if she'd move out of the way. She didn't. She'd been around the four-legged creatures long enough to know she had nothing to fear.

But she'd never seen anything like this one that was pawing the ground. He almost resembled an Andalusian, except he had the head of a cow pony, and those eyes…

"Is his name Trigger?" she asked as he tapped the ground with his right hoof.

"No, Buttercup."

Buttercup. *Right.* Only in the movies did horses come to their master's call. And even then they only did so because some poor sod was behind the cameras with a bucket of grain. Clinton had no such bucket. He calmly walked up to his mount, slipped the metal pipe he'd used to repair the fence into a leather sheath, then mounted up.

"Where are you going?"

Just then it started to rain, not tiny droplets of water, either, but fat globules that soaked her blouse almost instantly.

"That lightning cloud will be overhead before you know it. Best I get my horse under cover." He tipped his hat at her. "Pleasure meeting you, ma'am."

And then Clinton McAlister rode off, not into the sunset, but into the torrential downpour of a thunderstorm.

Chapter Two

When it rained in Montana, it *rained,* Clinton thought, keeping to a slow trot. Of course, he'd been born and raised in this country and so that came as no surprise.

But it might to the woman he'd left by the roadside. He found himself glancing back, the pool that had already gathered on the brim of his hat streaming in rivulets onto his shirt. Should have brought a jacket. But his soaked clothes didn't prevent him from pulling back on the reins for an instant. His horse obediently halted. He turned his horse's head just in time to hear her car door pop open. She disappeared from view.

At least one of them would stay dry.

I know about the mustangs.

Well, he thought, good for her. Knowing about the mustangs and being able to confirm their existence were two different things. Sure, there were those who'd come to the ranch in the hopes of seeing them. Amongst horse enthusiasts the Baer Mountain Mustangs were an urban legend. But the truth was, they weren't truly wild. The Baer family had kept them contained—and more or less hidden—for nearly two hundred years. Still, word had leaked out. People begged to see them or to help protect them or to film them…. He'd lost count of how many had come before her. And no matter who they might be or how much money they might offer him, he refused to confirm the urban legend was true. That was all he needed: a bunch of horse enthusiasts knocking on his door.

"Come on," he told Buttercup—yes, Buttercup— a private joke between him and his grandmother. "Let's head back to the ranch before we get washed down a canyon."

The gray gelding obediently moved into a canter, the gait as smooth as a carousel horse, or so his niece assured him. He never bothered to pull his horse's mane short and it flicked his hand with each tug of the horse's legs. It might be colder than the lair of a snake, but he loved riding in the rain. Thunder boomed overhead. Electricity charged the air and Clint found himself on the verge of a smile.

"Easy there," he told his horse who flicked its head up in response to the steady rumble. "We'll be back at the ranch in a minute."

There was a small rise straight ahead, and beyond that, another one. But he paused at the top of the first hill, and despite telling himself not to, he headed back to the road. Through streamers of rain, he could see the fuzzy outline of taillights.

She was going toward the ranch.

"Crap," he muttered. He watched for a second longer, waiting to see if she made a U-turn. She didn't. After a minute or two, she disappeared over another hill.

Now what? Did he go back to the house? Sure as certain, she'd be there, bugging him, asking about his herd of horses. Blah, blah, blah....

He just about rode in the other direction.

Instead he spurred his horse into a faster canter. If he hurried, he'd beat her back.

The ranch was surrounded by rolling hills and as he came down a softly sloping incline, he could just make out her car's headlights. It still rained, and by now, he was soaked to the bone, but it didn't bother him. What bothered him was the woman who hadn't taken "no" for an answer.

"Careful," he told Buttercup as his horse's front hooves lost purchase on the slick ground. They slid for a bit, leaving twin furrows in the soggy ground.

In the valley below, if one wanted to label it a valley because it was really more of a shallow bowl, sat the Baer Mountain Ranch. Two hundred years before, the main home had been nothing more than a one-room shack. Over the past hundred years, that'd changed. The home had morphed from a single room into a more conventional two-story ranch house. Nothing ostentatious—that wasn't the Baer family way—but it was a good-sized property, surrounded by various outbuildings. A three-story, three-sided metal hay barn stood off in the distance. Another metal shed that stored various farm equipment sat alongside it. A larger wooden structure that was a two-story horse stable was left of the house. Behind the barn, near the back pasture they'd carved a pad for an arena that was ringed by two-inch pipes. Various corrals attached to the side of it accommodated still more horses as well as cattle. It was, to outsiders, a normal ranch. And for the most part, that's exactly what it was. But the rest of it—the horses in the rugged mountains to the east—that was something he'd never talk about.

Not even to a good-looking, sweet-eyed interloper.

A horse out in pasture neighed as he approached the twelve-stall barn, Clint thinking absently that he and a few of the guys would need to buck some hay into the second-story loft pretty soon. Maybe he could get started on that task right now. That way, he could avoid the pretty little brunette pulling into the circular driveway. Point of fact, she'd arrived ahead of him, and, since he didn't see her in her car, he assumed Gigi had let her in.

Terrific, he thought, hopping off and tugging the reins over his horse's head right as another clap of thunder rang out. That meant he'd be forced to be nice to her. Although maybe not. Maybe she'd be gone by the time he untacked. Gigi could be a real pit bull if she didn't like someone.

The rain came down harder, hitting the tin roof of the barn like a million shards of glass. He took his time even though he'd started to grow cold in his soaked-to-the-bone shirt. The double doors to the barn afforded him a partial view of the front of the house. Nobody drove away.

"Damn," he muttered, unclipping his horse from the cross-ties when the cold became too much to bear. "Don't get comfortable in there," he told Buttercup as he let him loose in his stall. "I'll be back out when this rain stops."

She wasn't gone.

He saw her car the instant he stepped out of the barn. To be honest, that kind of stunned him. They didn't usually get many visitors in these parts, and when they did, Gigi usually sent them on their way damn quickly— especially if they were asking about the mustangs. For a second or two he hung back. The white window trim around the two-story home had turned gray from the rain. The yellow daisies Gigi loved and that she'd planted along the front porch were bowing their heads in protest. Clint stared at the front door as if expecting it to open at any moment. It didn't.

"Double damn." Guess he was stuck.

"Well, now," a familiar voice cried the second he

entered. He could smell brownies in the air, and that nearly brought him up short.

Gigi made brownies for treasured friends, for family and for important guests. None of which described their visitor. Then again, maybe Gigi had put them in the oven before the woman arrived.

"Clinton McAlister, what the devil's taken you so long out in that barn?"

"Horse's wet," he said, refusing to glance left in the direction of the family room. "Waited until he was dry."

He was certain his grandmother had her sitting on the floral-print couch beneath the front window. And he was certain they were both drinking tea, steam rising from a cup on the oak coffee table in front of them. He could smell the lemon from here. He hung his hat on a hook to the right. Water poured off the brim and landed on the hardwood floor.

"You better clean that up," his grandmother said, obviously spying the puddle.

"I know, I know..." he muttered, his spurs hitting the wood and emitting a chink-chink-chink as he walked toward the kitchen—and he still didn't shift his gaze in their guest's direction. He didn't *want* to. Peering into her attractive face affected him in a way that it probably shouldn't do given that they'd been strangers up until an hour ago.

"Come meet Samantha Davies."

"Already did," he said.

"Clinton!" his grandmother cried.

He about skidded to a stop.

"You sit down and be nice," Gigi ordered, and sure enough, she had her on the couch, one of his grand-mother's hands patting the seat cushion to the right of her. Their "guest" sat to her left.

And finally, reluctantly, he looked that woman in the eye. She was even prettier up close. Olive-colored skin. Brown hair that was short, but that flattered her high cheekbones and heart-shaped face. And eyes as green as springtime prairie grass.

"Gigi," he said to his grandmother, using the name he'd been calling her since he was three because he'd been unable to pronounce the words "Grandma Eugenia"; it'd all come out sounding like Gigigigi... and the name had stuck. "I need to go upstairs and change."

"Not before you shake hands," she said.

Fine, he told his grandmother with his eyes, the rowels of his spurs suddenly muffled when his muddy feet hit the area rug. She'd kill him later when she saw the brown spots.

"Clinton McAlister," he said, holding out his hand.

"Clint is my—"

"Ranch manager," he interrupted Gigi before she could say "grandson," which caused Gigi to draw back. For some reason, he didn't want this woman knowing who he was, although he wondered if she hadn't guessed already. This was a small town and people talked. Fact is, he owned the Baer Mountain Ranch. His grandmother had deeded it over to him a few years ago.

"Pleasure to meet you," he said, keeping their eye contact to a minimum.

Damn, but she was beautiful.

And warm. Her fingers were soft, her flesh so hot he nearly hissed.

"Clinton is actually—"

"Really cold," he interrupted his grandmother again, reluctantly releasing her hand. "As you can tell."

"Clinton," Gigi said, "whatever is the matter with you?"

If he admitted he was the owner of the Baer Mountain Ranch, he might be obligated to sit down and speak to this stranger—and that he didn't want to do. He had a feeling spending time with her would be... troublesome.

"I'm freezing, Gigi," he said. And then with his eyes he pleaded, *just humor me, would you?*

His grandmother might be pushing seventy, but she was no fool. She could smell something in the air...and it wasn't just brownies.

"Fine," she said. "Off with you. Go change." She waved her hands. "You smell like horse."

"Actually," their guest said before he could turn away, "I *like* the smell of horse."

Clint had no idea why the words sent a stab of warmth right through his gut. All she'd done was admit to something he understood—he liked the smell of horse, too. But hearing her softly feminine voice say the words *like* and *smell* in a sentence in connection to him, well, it made him think about stuff that he probably shouldn't, especially given that she'd been talking about *horses*.

"Well, I smell like *wet* horse," he said, more sternly than he meant to.

He caught his grandmother's gaze. She was leaning back now, her gray eyebrows lifted, and it was obvious she was trying not to smile.

"I'll be upstairs," he grumbled, turning.

"You'll go upstairs and change and then come right back downstairs," Gigi said.

"Gigi, I have work to do."

"That work can wait. It's still pouring outside."

It was, though it'd probably pass quickly. Storms this time of year always did.

"Go on," Gigi ordered, waving her hands again. "Mr. Ranch Foreman," she tacked on.

"Fine," he snapped.

Chapter Three

Samantha watched him go. Frankly, she was unable to tear her eyes away from him. The rain had turned his white shirt damn near transparent, and though her eyesight was failing, she could still make out every sinewy cord of muscle that rippled down his back.

"He's a real handful, that one," Eugenia Baer proclaimed.

Sam faced the woman she'd traveled two thousand miles to see. She hadn't expected to meet her. Everyone she'd ever talked to about Mrs. Baer had painted her a recluse. Although to be honest, the entire family was something of an enigma. If she'd had money to spare she could have hired a P.I. Instead she'd been forced to research on the Internet. Eugenia Baer appeared to be the last living descendant of William Baer, the man who'd founded the ranch.

"I don't think he wants me here," Samantha said, running her fingers through her brown hair, but there was hardly any hair there. She hadn't gotten used to having it all buzzed off in the hospital.

"Nonsense, dear. He's just wet and cold and miserable."

He wasn't wet and cold and miserable when they'd first met. Frankly, he'd been hard and sweaty and hot…

Sam!

At some point in the future she would have no idea if a man was good-looking or not. She better enjoy it while she could.

"Has he worked for you long?" Sam asked, hearing footsteps above her head. It was a weird question to ask given that she suspected Clinton had worked for the ranch his entire life. He *was* this woman's grandson. But Sam wasn't thinking clearly. Up there, somewhere on the second floor, a man was stripping out of his clothes.

She swallowed, forced herself to meet Eugenia's eyes.

"Who, Clinton?" she asked, looking uncomfortable all of a sudden. "Well, uh. Yes. I guess you could say he has worked for me a long time. Practically his whole life."

There was something about the way the woman said the words that alerted Sam to the fact that Eugena Baer thought Sam was clueless about Clinton's true identity. Interesting.

"Does he help with the Baer Mountain Mustangs?" she boldly asked, hoping to startle a confession. She had broached the subject of the horses just before Clint had walked in and she'd yet to discover if Mrs. Baer would admit to the wild herd.

"Um, yeah," Eugenia said, bending forward and grabbing her cup of tea off the table, "about those mustangs."

And here it was, Sam thought. This was when Eugenia Baer would deny the Baer Mountain Mustangs were still alive. Although to be honest, Sam felt fortunate to have gotten this far. Telling Eugenia she'd driven two thousand miles because the dream of seeing the horses had been the one thing to help her through the loss of her mom and dad had touched the rancher. As it happened she, too, had suffered a loss: her son-in-law and daughter had passed away a few years back.

"I've heard the rumors about them, of course," Eugenia said now. "Most people in these parts have." She held a porcelain cup with tiny violets painted on the side and it somehow suited the woman whose gray hair and ivory skin appeared almost too delicate to belong to a rancher. "But whatever makes you think these mustangs even exist?"

And Samantha caught her breath. Not the brush-off she'd expected.

"My mother," she said.

"Your mother?" the woman asked.

Sam nodded. "Before she died, when I was a child, she would tell me bedtime stories about them."

Eugenia raised her eyebrows.

"My grandmother lived outside of Billings."

"I see," Eugenia said.

Sam almost added more, but how could she explain to this stranger how important this was to her? Horses has always been such a huge part of her life. Before her mom and dad had died, she'd shown on the American quarter horse circuit, coming close to winning a world title or two, despite her parents' limited budget. They'd supported her riding into adulthood—if not financially, then emotionally—and then the accident had brought her whole world crashing down. Now, here she was, on the Baer Mountain Ranch, determined to do something she and her mom had always pledged to do together. Track down those horses. Sure it was a long way to drive in the hopes of convincing someone to help her dream come true, but she was determined to try.

"Look, dear," Eugenia said, taking a sip of her tea before setting her cup back down with a near-silent *clink.* "I can't tell you how many people have come to our ranch for the same reason."

Sam grew motionless.

"Most people come here seeking answers for commercial reasons. But I don't think I've ever had someone show up here asking to see the horses because their mom told them bedtime stories."

Sam didn't say anything. Frankly, she was on the verge of tears. The accident was fresh in her memory, and she still hurt every time she thought about that day. Still missed her mom and dad more than anything else in the world. Missed their daily phone calls. Missed updating them on her horse's progress. Missed calling them just to talk. Still wished things had been different that day and that they hadn't…

No!

That was a dangerous direction to take, her psychologist had warned her. There was a reason she'd been left behind. She had to believe that.

"Tell me, dear, how did they die?"

Sam cleared her throat. It took a second or two for her to gather her composure enough to talk. Above, the sounds had stopped. She hoped that didn't mean Clint McAlister was on his way back down.

"Car accident," she said. "We were on our way back from watching *The Nutcracker* last December. We did that every year, you see, ever since I was a little girl. It was icy. And, well…"

She couldn't finish her sentence, didn't need to. Eugenia reached out and clasped her hands. Sam looked into her eyes, saw compassion there and the deep, deep understanding that only someone who'd lost a loved one could *ever* understand.

"I was…out of it for a while," Sam admitted, though

she never talked about the wreck. Not to anyone. Not to her former coworkers. Not even to her friends. And yet here she was confessing all to this perfect stranger. "When I woke up I was told my parents were dead."

Hot tears seared her cheek. "They were all I had, though I was closest to my mom. She shared my love of horses. Went to almost all of my horse shows…" She swallowed back more tears. "That's why this is so important to me."

Eugenia nodded. "I see," she said with another squeeze.

"You don't have to tell me about the mustangs if you don't want to," Sam said. "I respect your family's desire to keep them to yourself. I mean, if they really are a wild herd running free on your land, you managed to keep them a secret all these years. I don't think I'd want to share them with the outside world, either."

Eugenia didn't say anything, just stared at her, probing the very depth of Sam's soul.

"You know what? Forget that I ever came here. I'm so sorry I intruded. I realize now what a terrible imposition this is."

She got up.

"Where do you think you're going?" Eugenia asked.

And Samantha's heart stopped.

"You sit down, young lady."

Sam sank onto the couch.

"You drive a hard bargain, though," Eugenia said.

"I do?" Sam asked.

"And I might have gotten crotchety in my old age, my grandson will tell you that, but even I'm not proof against such a request."

"Are they real?" she asked, her voice close to a whisper.

Eugenia's smile lit up the room. "What would you say if I told you they just might be?"

"I would say that's all I needed to hear." She started to stand again. But before she could turn away, Eugenia caught her hand.

"They're real," she said softly.

Samantha started to cry.

Oh, Mom. They really do exist.

She wished her mother was with her.

He walked into a damn therapy session—at least that's what it felt like what with everyone looking misty-eyed.

"What the hell happened?" Clinton burst out.

The two women glanced up. Samantha slowly sank back down to the couch. And then they were holding hands. Worse, he recognized the expression on his grandmother's face: she wanted to pull Samantha Davies into her arms.

"Go on with you," his grandmother said, releasing one of Samantha's hands and wiping her own eyes. "We were just having a little heart-to-heart."

"About what?" he asked.

"Our mustangs."

And if Clinton had been near that damn couch, he'd have sank into it, too. Never. Not once. Not in all the years that he'd been alive, had his grandmother ever admitted to a stranger that their mustangs were more than local legend.

"Gigi," he said gently.

"Sit down, *Mr. McAlister,*" she said, patting the couch. "We need to talk."

"About what?" he asked, preferring to move forward and sit in one of two armchairs across from them.

"Don't play stupid, young man. You'll be gathering our horses next week. I want you to take Samantha here along."

Samantha gasped. "Oh, Mrs. Baer. I can't do that!"

"Why not?"

"It's too much of an imposition."

Well, at least one of them was acting sensibly. "Gigi, please," he said. "She's right. It's not feasible, not to mention that it's highly dangerous. Why, can she even ride?"

She could be a reporter, he thought to himself. Or some kind of damn animal rights activist. Lord. The possibilities were endless.

"Don't be ridiculous," his grandmother said. "Of course she can ride. She's from the east coast." She said it as if everyone in that part of the country rode horses.

"What the blazes does that have to do with whether she can ride or not?"

"But I *can* ride," Samantha said in a small voice.

Clinton leaned back. He stared at the two women in front of him. Somehow, Samantha Davies had managed to wrap his grandmother around her little finger…and he wished he could figure out how she'd done it in such a short amount of time.

"I won't do it," he said. "I won't bring her along. It's too dangerous."

"Poppycock," Gigi said.

"Gigi, think about this. We don't even *know* this woman."

"She has a big heart," Gigi said, taking the woman's hand. "I can see it in her eyes."

"Thank you," Samantha said.

Clint released a sigh of frustration. "I'm telling you, Gigi, she might end up getting hurt. The spring gathering is tough. The weather's unpredictable." He motioned outside where the sun had started to pop through the clouds, the unsettled pattern typical for this time of year.

"It's a long ride. She'd have blisters on her bottom in two hours flat."

"Excuse me," Sam said. "I'm right here in the room with you and I assure you, I can ride. I can ride really, really well," she punctuated. "No blisters would be sprouting on *this* bottom." She smiled.

He ignored it. "Oh, yeah? Should we just take your word for that?"

"Of course not," she said. "You have horses here, right? Test me. Right now, if you like."

"Excellent idea," Gigi said, standing. "Let's go."

"Gigi," Clint said, "this is crazy."

"It's not crazy," his grandmother said. "At least no more crazier than anything you've done in recent days, Mr. Ranch Manager. I want to do this." She glanced in Samantha Davies's direction. "For her."

Clinton didn't have a choice. "Hell's fires," he muttered. This day just got better and better.

Chapter Four

Clinton stormed out of the house, so upset he nearly slammed the door.

"Damn, foolish women."

Gigi had insisted Samantha go and change, which meant Clint had been left with the task of fetching her suitcase. "Of all the stupid, ridiculous ideas. Probably wants me to go saddle up a horse, too," he grumbled under his breath.

As it turned out, that's exactly what his grandmother asked him to do.

"Please," Gigi added with a smile. Clint stared between his grandmother and his "guest" and envisioned a cartoon character of himself—one with an angry red light shooting up his face like a thermometer.

"Sure," he said sarcastically, having to resist the urge to slam the door a second time.

The rainstorm had passed—gone as quickly as it'd come. He paused for a second in the barn's aisle. He wanted to saddle up the rankest bronc he could find, but as much as he was tempted, he wouldn't do that. He didn't want to kill the woman, no matter that she'd seriously pissed him off by batting her big green eyes at his grandmother. It didn't matter that he owned the ranch, either, and that he had every right to tell Samantha Davies to get lost. He wouldn't do *that,* either, because the plain and simple truth was, he loved his grandmother. He would do anything for her. She knew it, too. Gigi Baer had been a rock in his life and if she wanted Miss Samantha Davies to go along on the spring gathering, he'd let her go along.

If she could ride.

He wouldn't compromise her safety, the safety of his men and the safety of his livestock just because some city slicker had a wild hair up her you-know-what.

"Oh!" he heard his grandmother say when less than ten minutes later, the two of them, Samantha and his grandmother, entered the barn, their footfalls clearly audible on the packed dirt. "You've saddled Red."

Clint was tightening the girth—Red on cross ties in the middle of the aisle—the smooth leather strap Clint held gliding through the metal ring. Samantha now wore jeans, he saw, and a light green shirt.

"She said she could ride." Red was at least sixteen hands, and about as wide as he was tall, too. Lots of power.

When he glanced up, Samantha was staring at him. Horses chomped on the midafternoon snack he'd given them, their softly muffled snorts breaking the silence, and he thought to himself that she didn't seem afraid of Red at all. She came right up to him, offering the palm of her hand for the horse to sniff.

"Hey there, Red," she said softly.

The horse started to nibble at her palm—as if trying to eat an invisible treat.

"Do you happen to have an English saddle?" she asked, green eyes shifting in his direction.

"Excuse me?" he asked, leather girth forgotten.

She was backlit, her short brown hair blond around the

edges. "I usually ride English," she said with a wide I-know-that-might-sound-strange smile. "The truth is, I can count on one hand how many times I've ridden western."

He dropped the strap, rested his arm on the chestnut horse's withers and met his grandmother's gaze. "You hear that, Gigi? The woman wants to ride in an English saddle."

His grandmother just shook her head. It was cool inside the barn, a gentle breeze blowing up the aisle. Gigi had tossed a tan jacket over her white blouse and jeans.

"Just finish saddling that horse, Clint. If she's been riding English, a western saddle ought to be a piece of cake."

Clint shrugged. "Suit yourself," he said, and went back to girthing up the horse, wrapping the strap in and out of the metal loop before giving it a final tug. He'd hung the left stirrup over the saddle horn to keep it out of his way while he worked, but he released it quickly—too quickly—the thing slapping against Red's wide body. The horse pinned his ears.

"Maybe I can send for my own saddle if things work out," she told his grandmother, smiling sheepishly.

Only if she managed to control the horse beneath *this* saddle. But he found himself snorting nonetheless. The ranch hands would laugh themselves silly if they caught sight of someone riding one of his cow ponies in an English saddle.

Over his dead body.

"Excuse me," he said, eyeing the tack room behind her. "I need to get Red's bridle."

"Oh," she said, taking a step back.

But it wasn't enough.

He brushed past her, Samantha's gaze darting to his body like a foam bullet from a Nerf gun. "Sorry," she said.

He paused for a heartbeat. Their arms had touched. That was all. It wasn't as if his crotch had accidentally crossed one of her no-fly zones. Yet it felt as if that's exactly what happened. Worse, he felt a familiar buzz in that same region.

Crap.

He didn't look at her, but he couldn't deny that he fought the urge to glance back as he stepped into the tack room. The smell of leather filled his nostrils, it was such a familiar scent that it instantly soothed him.

"Just been without a woman too long," he muttered to himself. "Nothing to it."

He grabbed the bridle from the rack, turned.

Gigi stood there.

"What was that you were saying?" she asked. The look on her face was the same one he recognized from years of stepping in cow patties—and then entering her house afterward.

"I said it's been too long since I've cleaned this bridle."

That's not what you said, his grandmother silently told him.

That's my story and I'm stickin' to it, he told her right back on his way out.

The snaffle bit was the only piece of English tack he owned. Thing was, old Red wasn't very responsive to the jointed piece of metal. But if she knew how to ride…

Red stood still as he slipped the leather halter off his head, the big horse opening his mouth obediently. The metal mouthpiece clinked against his teeth, but it didn't bug the sorrel gelding. They were used to that kind of thing, just as they were used to the leather headstall being tugged over their ears. Once he buckled the throat-latch, he stepped back.

"He's all yours," he said with a smile as false as their ancient ranch hand Elliot's fake teeth.

"Thanks," she said, reaching for the reins. She stepped up to Red's left side, the correct side to lead a horse from, but not something a greenhorn would know. Clint had his first inkling that she might know a thing or two.

"I saw an arena out behind the barn. Should I take him there?"

"Sure," Gigi said.

Clint glanced at his grandmother, who shot Clint an I-told-you-so grin. This time it was Clint who shook his head.

There was at least an inch of water on the ground, the horse's hooves sucking at the earth in rhythmic plop-plop-plops. But it was still cool outside and that might present a problem, too. Cool weather was like a drug to horses—uppers. They could be slightly rambunctious after a cooldown like they'd just had.

But Samantha Davies opened the arena gate without the slightest hesitation, yet another clue that she knew her way around a ranch. Most gates were made with the same type of latch. Someone who wasn't familiar with them wouldn't know how they worked, but she flipped the latch and then slid it loose with an expert turn of the wrist.

Maybe he should have come up with another test. Like trick riding or calf roping or something.

She closed the gate behind her as easily as she opened it. There was no fear on her face as she turned to Red, just obvious determination as she lifted her foot into the stirrup. Her jeans pulled tight across her bottom, and Clint found himself staring at the shape of her rear until Gigi nudged him in the side.

"What?" he asked as Samantha Davies expertly pulled herself into the saddle.

"I think you really *have* been without a woman for too long," Gigi said with a wicked smile, and then— God help him—a wink.

"WHERE TO?" SAMANTHA ASKED, picking up the slack on the reins and turning Red toward the rail. "You want me to do some figure eights or something?"

Eugenia Bear had a grin on her face about as wide as the snow-capped mountains behind her. "Can you do a reining pattern?" she asked.

"Gigi," her grandson said. "She said she rides English. She doesn't know what a reining pattern is."

"Actually, I do," Sam said, trying to keep the wattage of her grin down. "I've watched more than my fair share at horse shows. I bet if you ran some of those cows over there into the arena, I could do some cutting for you, too."

Eugenia's pleasure appeared to grow—if possible. "There," she said to Clinton, "you see? She's an expert."

"So she claims," he said. "But I'd like to actually see her do the pattern before we move on to cows—*if* we move on to cows."

"Well, I don't know the pattern, exactly," Sam said, "but I have a pretty clear idea what to do. Let's see what I can get this little cow pony to do."

"Little?" she heard Clint huff.

"Most of the horses I ride are closer to seventeen hands," she said. "They breed them big on the quarter horse circuit."

She pulled Red away before she could gauge Clint's reaction. A reigning pattern was meant to showcase a rider's ability to control a horse. Those patterns were always performed in a western saddle, but that wouldn't matter. Patterns had been a big part of her training, and that gave her confidence as she guided Red toward the rail.

"Come on," she told the horse. "You gotta make me look good."

But Red didn't like to go. That became apparent the instant she tried to squeeze him into a canter—or a *lope*—as the western people labeled it. He didn't even want to trot, much less jog—or God forbid—gallop. But she hadn't ridden over fences for nothing. Holding on over three-foot obstacles, sometimes higher, had given her the legs of a linebacker. She ground her heels into Red and *made* him behave.

He did.

Sam sighed. There was nothing, absolutely nothing, like riding a horse. She hadn't ridden much in the past few months—doctor's orders—but it was a lot like roller skating. Once you knew how, you never forgot.

"Okay," she called out, trying to ignore the saddle horn as she squeezed Red. English saddles didn't have horns and so she was somewhat distracted by its presence. "Here I go."

The pattern was deceptively simple. Big circle at a lope, change of pace, then a small circle. Switch leads. Do the same thing going the other direction. Stop in the middle. Spin. Red didn't like the spin, but she dug her leg into him and made him do it. All in all, it wasn't a bad pattern, and she loved the last part where she got to run down the middle of the arena at a full gallop, coming to a sliding stop at the end. That part Red did beautifully.

"Bravo!" Eugenia called out when she was done. "That was terrific."

Perhaps not terrific, Sam thought, but she gave Red a pat on the neck nonetheless. They'd hardly win points on the quarter horse circuit, but she was proud of her ride and, man, it felt *wonderful* to be back, almost as wonderful as the look on Clint's face.

"I bet I really *could* work some of those cows," Sam said, riding up to where her audience stood.

"How long has it been?" Eugenia said.

"Not since the accident," she said. She hadn't had the heart when they'd finally given her the go-ahead, not when she was going to have to sell her horse anyway to cover her medical bills.

Coaster, her beloved black gelding, was going to a new home soon.

"Accident?" Clint asked. "What accident?"

"The one that killed my parents," Sam admitted.

Chapter Five

Her parents were dead?

"What?" Clint asked.

"They died four months ago," she said. "Just before Christmas."

Damn. No wonder Gigi had taken an instant shining to her. His grandmother's maternal instincts were legendary. Crap. It's what'd gotten him through the death of his own parents.

Gigi had never truly recovered from the death of her only child. To be honest, Clint had never truly recovered, either. Even though he'd lost his mom and dad years ago—ten, to be exact—he still missed them every day of his life.

"I'm sorry," he said, his gut twisting as he recalled his own grief. "I know what that's like. It's not easy."

She nodded, Red shifting beneath her, but she controlled the horse beautifully. He was an honest man—something he prided himself on—and she had one of the nicest seats he'd seen on a woman in a long time, and he wasn't talking about the seat she sat on. Although that was nice, too.

"You should stay with us."

Clint jerked his head up. He'd been leaning against

the top rail of the gate and he damn near stumbled backward when he heard Gigi say the words.

"What?" Samantha asked.

Gigi nodded toward the woman on horseback. "You should say with us," she said again. "You can help us prep for the gathering in a few days."

"Gigi," Clint said in a low, furious voice, hoping the woman behind him was hard of hearing. "Are you crazy? We just met her today."

"Clinton McAlister," Gigi said, turning toward him. "I can't believe you would say that. Just look into that child's eyes. She's still grieving." And this time it was his grandmother who lowered her voice. "And you know better than most what that's like. Don't be a complete ass."

Ass?

His grandmother spent entirely too much time on the Internet.

"Fine," he said, because what else could he say? If he kept on protesting he would, indeed, end up looking like an ass. "But she stays in one of the bunkhouses."

His grandmother shook her head. "The boys'll be using that next week. She can't be staying in a bunkhouse with men. She'll stay in the house."

"Gigi!"

"Don't you Gigi me," she said, wagging a finger at him. "I've swatted your butt a time or two before and I'm not afraid to do it again."

"Wait." Gigi and Clint turned to face Samantha. "You don't need to open up your home to me, Mrs. Baer."

Her home? It was *his* home. But, of course, Samantha didn't know that. Or maybe she did. Frankly, he didn't care. She couldn't stay with them. That was that.

"Don't be silly," Gigi said. "If you're going on the

roundup, you'll need to stay here. We don't leave until later this week and there isn't a hotel within twenty miles."

"Yes, but—"

"I won't take *no* for an answer," Gigi said, holding up a hand.

He would take *no*. "Gigi—"

"You can sleep upstairs," she added. "In the room next to mine."

"Gigi," he repeated, and then lowered his voice. "Don't be ridiculous. There's plenty of other rooms for her to choose from."

Which gave his Gigi the wrong impression; that he was okay with Samantha staying with them.

"Fine," Gigi said, a smile settling upon her face. Obviously, she felt as if she'd won this particular battle. "You can pick your room, Samantha," she said.

"Call me Sam," the woman on horseback said with a smile. "Nobody calls me Samantha except used car salesmen and telephone solicitors."

"Sam," his grandmother said, "there's plenty to choose from."

"Well, I—" she started to say, until Red put his head down and let loose a snort that drowned out her words.

"What was that, dear?" Gigi asked.

"I think she said no," Clint pointed out.

"Actually, I said I don't want to *impose*," Sam explained, pulling on the reins because Red was trying to sniff the sand in the arena.

"You wouldn't be imposing. We'd love to have you, wouldn't we, Clinton?" Gigi asked.

"Oh, yeah," Clint said jovially. "I'd *love* to have you."

His grandmother elbowed him again, the expression on her adorably wrinkled face clearly warning him to behave.

"I just don't think it's a smart idea," Sam said.

"Clinton," his grandmother said, "now that that's settled, why don't you untack Red here? I'll show Sam to the house."

"Gigi, she just said she didn't think it was a smart idea."

"Nonsense. Sam, hop on down from there. Clint can take care of Red."

"But, I—"

"Best do as she asks," Clint advised. "Once she gets an idea in her head, you're not going to get it out."

"Are you sure?" she asked Gigi.

"I'm sure, honey. Now hop on down from there."

"But I can untack him." Sam slipped out of the saddle.

"Excellent idea," Clint said with his own bright smile—though his was false. Okay, maybe not false, more like wolfish. He'd spotted the blush on Samantha's face, the one that had flared at his "I'd *love* to have you" comment. "Maybe we can both do it *together*."

"Clinton," his grandmother snapped in warning. "Quit teasing her. You're making her uncomfortable."

Obviously, his grandmother had spotted the blush on Samantha's face, too. He looked at Gigi in question. He hadn't seen her so protective in…well, he couldn't remember when she'd taken someone under her wing so thoroughly, and in such a short amount of time. She must like Samantha Davies a lot. Then again, he supposed that was to be expected. He and Gigi had been through more than their fair share of grief. First his parents, then her own husband five years ago to a heart attack. His grandmother had deeded the ranch to him, she'd been so stricken by grief. For a time there, Clint wasn't sure she'd make it through. But she'd managed to recover. And now she had that light back in her eyes.

"I'm sure Sam's tired from her drive. You can take care of the horse."

"That's okay, Mrs. Baer, I can do it myself—"

"Gigi," his grandmother said. "Everyone calls me that."

Everyone? The only person to call her that was him.

"Gigi, I'd really like to untack and brush him myself."

"She could untack and brush me," Clint said under his breath.

His grandmother shot him a look and muttered out of the side of her mouth, "What you're after is a piece of ass, and don't think I don't know it."

"Gigi!" Clint said, pretending to be horrified. He opened the gate for Sam and smiled up at her. "Seriously," he said to Samantha, "I'll help you out."

Maybe he could scare her into going away.

SHE COULD UNTACK AND BRUSH ME.

Had he been flirting with her when he'd said that? Somehow she doubted it. And why didn't he want her to know who he was? Earlier, when she'd been talking to his grandmother, it'd been clear that he'd wanted Eugenia to introduce him as a simple ranch hand…and not as his grandson.

Why?

"Clint," she said. "I, uh…I know you're Eugenia's grandson."

He stopped so suddenly Red tossed his head. "You do?"

She nodded.

"Did Gigi tell you?"

She shook her head. "I knew from the first moment I met you."

"Oh," he said. She could tell he was trying to hide his surprise from her.

Moisture still hung heavy in the air. A breeze played with her short hair and it blew the scent of him toward her.

He smelled like a man.

And she was attracted to that scent. It made her recall—perfectly—what he'd looked like with his shirt open. Those cords of muscle, the tan hue of his skin, the way she'd caught him looking at her earlier, as if he'd like to—

Sam!

"She's really a special lady," she said through a throat gone dry with—okay, she should just admit it—*lust*. She hadn't been with a man since the Mesozoic era.

"Yes, she is."

But she wasn't the type to indulge in an affair although if there was one time in her life when it might be okay to do something impulsive, that was now. Sex with him would be something to remember for a lifetime, and since she was going blind…

Blind.

She couldn't breathe for a moment, forced her lungs to pump air to her heart. The sad truth was that she *couldn't* imagine it. She could only try her best to prepare for it. She'd been left behind for some reason. She had to believe that reason would present itself at some point in the future.

Maybe it was the Baer Mountain Mustangs.

"Tell me about them," she said, their entrance into the barn giving Sam a second or two of panic when her vision dimmed. But it was only her eyes adjusting to the sudden darkness.

"Tell you about what?"

She led Red to the cross-ties. "The mustangs."

He didn't say anything. She swiveled around and grabbed Red's halter from the hook Clint had hung it on.

"Yeah," he said. "About the mustangs."

She slipped the bridle from Red's head, before turning back to him. The horse spat the bit out as if he was aiming for a spittoon.

"What about them?"

"Gigi can be too trusting sometimes. Gullible. Naive."

"So can we all," she said, remembering a time when she'd thought life would never change. It had only been last December. She was too young—just barely twenty-six. Her parents had still been young, too, and healthy. They'd had years ahead of them. Or so she'd thought, four months ago.

"She *likes* you," he said. "But the jury's still out as far as I'm concerned."

She slipped the halter over Red's head. "That's not what it seemed like earlier," she said as she buckled the crown piece. Though she was losing more and more of her peripheral vision, she'd been having trouble focusing up close, too. She worried about what that might mean, then shook her head. What did she have to fear? That she was going blind? She already knew that for sure.

Enjoy every day.

Her doctor's words echoed in her ears. She *would* enjoy every day. That was going to be her motto from here on out. So when she finished, she faced Clint with more bravado than she truly felt. Maybe it was the gut-wrenching realization that she would be unable to see him in the not-too-distant future. Maybe it boiled down to good, old-fashioned lust—God, she'd never forget what he looked like tapping that pole into the ground— but for some reason, she felt like playing with him.

"You mean you can take me to the mustangs, but then you'll have to kill me?"

"I, well, I—" He frowned. "No. Of course not. I'm just not taking you anywhere until your background checks out."

"So you're going to do a background check on me?" she said, closing the distance between them. He seemed to lean away from her. Or maybe he didn't. But his pupils flared, his chin lifting a bit when she got too close. Like a horse about to turn and run, Clint's muscles tensed. She could see the cords of his neck pop out, watched as his eyes narrowed.

She would never forget his luminescent blue eyes.

And *hungry.*

He was attracted to her.

"You could be a reporter for all I know," he said.

"I'm not."

"Just what are you then?" He scooted closer to *her,* turning the tables.

He leaned into her. Sam couldn't breathe. And then she sucked in a breath…and got a mouthful of musky-smelling Clinton McAlister.

"Who are you, Samantha Davies?"

Chapter Six

One of the horses snorted in the stall behind Sam. He saw her jump. She was on edge. Excellent. So was he.

"What do you do for a living?" he asked, staring into her big, green eyes. "So far all I know is that you ride horses." He smirked. "English."

"And that should reassure you," she said, lifting her chin. "I'm a horse person, and so I can't be half-bad." She patted Red.

He moved even closer, smiling when he saw her swallow. Hard.

"Yeah," he said softly, "but what do you *do* for a living?" he asked again. The question wasn't that hard. He must have her rattled.

"Nothing."

"Nothing?" he repeated, and he could swear he felt heat emanating from her all of a sudden. Her cheeks grew rosy, and then the color spread to her neck.

"I'm a geologist."

That caught him off guard. "A geologist?"

She shoved a strand of hair away from her eyes. The wind had mussed it up. "I put myself through school, found myself a high paying job. I used to work for one of the chemical companies."

"Used to? What happened? You get fired?" He wasn't thinking right. Under normal circumstances he would never ask such a rude question.

She must have *him* rattled.

"I had to quit. They gave me three months off to heal, longer if I needed it, but I'm still sort of recovering from my injuries. Plus, I started having issues at work, couldn't focus…so I quit."

"Quit and came here."

She nodded.

"But you said you have a horse. One that you used to show."

"I *do* have a horse, but he's for sale down in Texas."

"You don't strike me as the type that would want to sell her horse."

She shrugged. "My medical bills, the portion that the insurance company didn't cover. It was expensive. My horse is worth a lot of money. I have to do what I can to pay the bills."

So she was selling her horse. The only thing she owned, if he didn't miss his guess.

The whole story kind of made him sick. And what injuries was she still recovering from? She looked fine to him.

"You should probably get going before Gigi comes out here and tans my hide for keeping you too long."

"Yeah, you're probably right," she said, hooking the left stirrup over the horn of the saddle so she could undo the girth.

"I thought you didn't know how to ride western?" he asked, resting a hand on Red's neck.

"I said I didn't ride in a western saddle, but that doesn't mean I don't know how the saddles work."

Despite himself, his gaze drifted downward to her

rear. The memory of how it'd felt to have her be the aggressor, however briefly, made his body react in a way that made him uncomfortable given that he'd just met her.

She glanced at him—and caught him still staring at her behind.

A smile slowly lifted the edges of her mouth. "Do I have dirt on me?" she asked.

He knew she knew exactly what he'd been doing: checking her out. But that didn't seem to bother her, and for the first time he found himself thinking that it might not be a bad thing that she was staying in the house.

"Your rear looks great to me," he said, throwing caution to the wind.

"So does yours."

"You sure you don't want to bunk down in the room next to me?"

He'd pushed too far. He could tell by the way the back of her neck turned red and she suddenly devoted all her attention to Red. "No thanks," she said as she pulled the heavy leather saddle toward her.

But a western saddle was not an English saddle and she began to tip backward under the weight of it.

"Careful," he called, reaching out to help her. He pushed the saddle back on Red's back just in time, and when he turned to steady her, they were belly-to-belly, Clint's hands clutching her upper arms.

"Uh…thanks," she said. "I, uh…I lost my balance."
Let her go.

"Western saddles are heavy," he murmured. Her arms were tiny. He could just about wrap his entire hand around one.

"Yeah. I just thought…" He held her gaze.

Let. Her. Go.

"What'd you think?" he asked softly. Just touching

her about lit him on fire and he couldn't imagine what it'd be like to kiss her—

"Gracious! You're still in here."

They sprang apart.

Gigi stared at him in silent rebuke. "What the devil's taking so long, Clint? Her tea's getting cold."

"DON'T LET HIM PUSH YOU around," Gigi told Sam as she led her away from the barn.

"Believe me, I won't," the young woman said, her eyes peering down at the ground.

"Do you have a hotel back in town?" Gigi asked. "Do you need to go back there and check out?"

"No, but really, Mrs. Baer, I hate to impose."

She seemed like such a sweet thing. Gigi had wanted to wrap her up and tell her everything would be all right. Samantha had a world of hurt hiding inside.

"It's fine," Gigi said. "But you'll need to watch that one in there," she said, pointing over her shoulder. "He's a real scallywag."

She glanced back at the barn. "I've noticed."

"He thinks because he's my grandson he can boss me around."

"I've noticed that, too."

Gigi studied her. "So I take it that means you knew who he was this whole time. My grandson. Not some kind of ranch hand."

"I knew," she said.

Clever girl. "Well, thank God for that. With Clint admitting he lives with me, I was hoping you didn't think me a cougar or something."

The young woman stared at her for long seconds, but then threw back her head and laughed. It was so good to see her let loose. She had a feeling that hadn't happened in a while. And, my, but she was a handsome thing. No wonder Clint was interested in her, although to be honest, Clint had had plenty of beautiful women throwing themselves at him in the past. Not that Sam had thrown herself at him. Quite the opposite, in fact. It was just strange that her grandson was showing an interest in the girl when he'd just met her.

Strange and encouraging. She'd given up all hope of ever having great-grandchildren.

"I wouldn't have thought that. Well, maybe I might have," she said. "But only for about one-point-nine seconds."

"Well," Gigi said, "as long as it wasn't for *two* seconds, I would have forgiven you."

It'd been too long since Clint had shown interest in any girl, Gigi thought. Oh, there'd been the odd trip into town. He was, after all, a man. But not since Julia had he been so obvious in his pursuit.

Julia. God. Now there was a woman she'd been glad to see the last of.

She can bunk down next to me.

Gigi just bet her grandson would like that.

"It's a beautiful house," Sam said, stopping yet again and gazing up at it.

She loved horses. She'd be *perfect* for Clint.

"It's been in my family for a long, long time," Gigi said.

But she was from the city and so that might be a problem. It'd been a problem with Julia. And that made Clint's interest in Sam all the more strange. Gigi would have thought after Julia he'd give a woman like Sam a wide berth.

"That's right," Sam said. "Your family settled this land in the early eighteen-hundreds."

Maybe he was just flirting with her. Maybe that's all this was.

"We were one of the first families to live in Montana," she said. "That's how we ended up with so much acreage."

"Twelve thousand acres."

"No, dear," Eugenia said. "That's just this parcel here." She motioned to the land around them. "We own another hundred thousand to the west there."

"Really? I only ever read about the twelve thousand acres online."

She hadn't known that? Good. At least Gigi wouldn't have to worry about Sam wanting Clinton for his money…like she had with Julia. It was obvious Sam had been attracted to her grandson before she'd known what he was worth.

"And another fifty-thousand to the east. We have some smaller parcels in between that."

"I had no idea," Sam mused.

"We're one of the largest landowners in Montana." She watched the woman's eyes carefully, looking to see if a glint of something entered them. Maybe greed, or delight, or the conniving machination of a woman after her grandson for what he was worth on paper… which was a lot.

"That's how you've kept the horses a secret all these years, isn't it?" she asked.

So far, so good. The girl didn't seem the least little bit gleeful.

"We move them around a lot," Gigi admitted, "which is why they're not truly wild. We manage them just like we do the cattle."

"So they don't run free in the hills?"

Gigi shook her head. "If we let them to do that they'd

quickly reproduce in such numbers that they'd become a problem. So we selectively allow them to breed."

"Oh," she said, disappointed.

"But they run free on *a lot* of land," Gigi added.

"I see."

One of the first questions out of Julia's mouth was exactly how many acres did they own.

"We run cattle here, too," Gigi said. "It's how we keep the place afloat. We might be rich in land, but we have to make ends meet somehow. Some years, it's not easy what with the cattle market being up and down. We've thought about selling some of our land, but then what would we do with the horses?"

That wasn't true. That wasn't true *at all,* but if Sam here was after Clint's wealth, like Julia had been, Gigi wanted to know about it. So she watched Sam's face closely for signs.

She just looked sad.

"Have you ever thought about setting up a trust for the horses?" Sam asked. "You know, maybe gather together some private investors. I've met a lot of wealthy people—through showing horses—and so I could probably coordinate it all. That way, when money is tight, you wouldn't have to worry about caring for the horses again."

"No," Gigi said honestly. Because in truth the Baers were wealthy. *Very* wealthy. They'd sold land over the years, invested it. Yes, they lived simply, hadn't remodeled the house in the past fifty years, or added expensive horse barns or flaunted their wealth. No need for that. They kept to themselves.

"I'd like to help," Sam said, "if you'll let me. Horse people are great. If I tell them I need money for wild mustangs, they'll be onboard. It'll be a tax write-off for them. That'll be a plus. And if they donate money we could generate annual income. That income would grow over the years. You guys would never have to worry about taking care of your horses again."

And in that instant, Gigi made her decision: Samantha Davies would marry her grandson.

"That's a *fine* idea," Gigi said.

But she wasn't talking about horses, she was talking about her grandson's upcoming marriage to Sam.

Chapter Seven

Clint knew something was up the second he entered the house. "Where is she?" he asked Gigi.

"Upstairs." She reached for a piece of bread, which she lay on a cutting board. Looked like turkey sandwiches for lunch. "Settling into her room."

"The one next to mine?" he asked sarcastically.

"No. The one next to *mine,*" Gigi said, glancing up, a piece of lettuce in her hand. She wore an apron with a skull and crossbones on it, the skull wearing a chef's hat. It'd been a Christmas present three years ago. "You will leave that girl alone, Clinton."

It was hard to take a woman seriously when she wore something that said: My Cooking's To Die For.

"Or what, Grandma Gigi?" he asked, plopping down on the kitchen chair that was already cocked in her direction.

"Or I'll lock you in your room."

He smiled, stretched his arms up behind him and yawned before saying, "You gonna ground me?" Gigi's habit of treating him like a little boy was a running joke between them.

"I'm going to put a lock on her door, that's what I'm

going to do. Don't think I didn't hear you in that tack room. You want that girl."

"And if I do?" he asked. "What's wrong with that? You like her, don't you? Cripes, you told her about the horses."

"I *do* like her. She's been through so much, poor thing. And the horses obviously mean a lot to her. She's not going to do anything to harm them."

"How do we know that?" he asked. "I mean, really, Gigi, what do we know about her? She shows up on our doorstep, unannounced. Doesn't call beforehand. Doesn't do anything but show up here claiming to be a geologist—"

"She's a geologist?"

"She *was.* Guess she had to quit. But that's beside the point. We don't know anything about her."

"I ran a Google search for her while you two were outside."

Clint rocked back in his chair.

Why was he *not* surprised?

Ever since he'd installed that damn satellite dish Gigi had spent more time on the Internet than she did outside. Well, maybe not really…but *still.*

"And what did Mr. Google say?" he asked, crossing his arms in front of him.

"She's an excellent rider," Gigi said.

"Yeah?"

Gigi nodded, popping open a tub of processed meat. "I didn't have time to scan for much, but what I found was impressive. She's ridden horses at quarter horse shows. There's pages and pages of horse show results where her name is listed. She's won numerous awards. There was even an article written about her. A 'hardworking amateur,' that's what they called her. They said she had to make a lot of sacrifices to keep on showing."

"Terrific," he said. "Great. But will she keep quiet about *our* horses?"

"I think so." But then she stopped what she was doing and slowly faced him. "I saw something about the accident, too."

"Oh, yeah?" He supposed it was sort of morbid to discuss that.

"It was a big deal where she lived. Made the local news. I guess she was in a coma."

I was out of it for a little while.

It appeared that had been an understatement. And though he didn't know Samantha Davies very well, he wouldn't be human if he didn't feel sorry for her. He couldn't imagine waking up in a hospital only to be told by a stranger your parents were dead. When they'd broken the news to him it'd come from Gigi.

"She was horribly sick. One of the local papers did a follow-up. The girl didn't wake up for two weeks. Missed her parents' funeral." Gigi shook her head. "According to the paper, she doesn't have family. The only people at the funeral were friends. Sad. *Very* sad."

Missed her parents' funeral? That had to have been tough. While the day he'd buried his parents had been one of the most difficult of his life, it had provided him a small amount of comfort to say a final goodbye.

"So you've convinced yourself we can trust her simply because of what she's been through?"

Gigi sucked something off her thumb—mustard by the looks of it. "I believe so," she said. "But there's no way to be certain." She leaned back against the counter. "One thing I can tell you, though, is that the girl's been through a lot. And really, when you think about it, what does it matter? We've been lucky to keep the mustangs a secret for this long. Sooner or later it was bound to get out."

"Yeah, but I'd just as soon delay the inevitable. I'm not looking forward to a bunch of crazy people knocking on our door. My biggest fear is that one day someone will get the idea to designate our horses as a national landmark or something. And then they'll impose all kinds of rules and restrictions on how we handle, care and manage them...even though they're *our* horses. Technically, we own them and so nobody can have a say in what we do with them. Still, I wouldn't put it past someone to try."

"Yeah, but maybe it's time we took our chances. I'm not getting any younger. And what if you never marry? What if we both die without someone to carry on the ranch? Wouldn't it be better to have something in place—maybe a trust like she was talking about—as insurance in case something like that happens?"

Clint could tell all this talk of death had gotten to her. He got up from his chair, snatched a sandwich from the cutting board, then bent and kissed Gigi's head. "Nothing's going to happen to either one of us, Gigi. Not for a long time."

But as he drew back and looked down at her, he noticed that her hair had gotten more gray in recent years; it was almost pure white now. And her face had more lines in it. And her eyes, once so full of life, looked tired.

"But what if it does?" she asked.

Or maybe she was merely sad—on Sam's behalf. He shook his head. "You're working yourself up over nothing. The horses will be fine. And if you trust this girl, then I'm willing to believe you, too, but you need to lay down some rules with her. Just because you like her doesn't mean we shouldn't take precautions."

"Okay," she said, smiling up at him.

Man, he loved his Gigi. He didn't know what he'd

have done without her all those years ago. The fact that there was a woman upstairs, one who'd just lost her parents, too, and that she'd had nobody to lean on after her parents' death…well, maybe it was fate that had brought her to their doorstep.

"Where you going?" she asked as he spun away while taking a bite of the sandwich.

"Gonna go see our new guest and lay down the law."

"Don't talk with your mouth full of food," she said, frowning.

"Well," he replied after swallowing, "don't ask me a question after I've taken a bite."

"Clint."

Reluctantly, he met her gaze.

"I mean it when I say stay away from her. Poor thing's been through enough. She doesn't need her life complicated by some weekend fling."

"By the sound of it, she's going to be here longer than a weekend."

His grandmother's eyes narrowed, lips pursed. "You know what I mean."

He knew. Of course he knew. And Gigi was right. "I promise to behave."

SAM CHANGED HER MIND ABOUT staying with Gigi at least a hundred times. As she unpacked her suitcase upstairs she kept thinking about Clint and what had happened—or had *almost* happened—in the barn. There'd been a second or two there, a brief instant, when she'd thought he might kiss her.

And she'd wanted him to.

Had her bump on the head caused her to lose her mind, too? She'd just *met* the man.

That more than anything made her doubt her decision

to stay. She would stop every once in a while, stare out the window—at the rolling green hills and the mountains in the distance—and wonder if she was doing the right thing. Her mother must be rolling over in her grave. The Davies family didn't take advantage of other people's wealth, and it was obvious the Baers were well off. Though they didn't live extravagantly, even the room was a testament to how comfortable a home they'd created. Done up in shades of off-white, it was the quintessential girl's room—right down to the umbrella-top lamp shade with tiny teardrop crystals dangling down. Yet here she was.

I'm going to see the Baer Mountain horses, Mom.

"You look like you're about ready to get a root canal."

Clint stood in the open door, the ultimate cowboy in his beige button-down, tan hat and tight, tight jeans.

Sam!

"Just thinking about my parents," she admitted absently, then immediately wished she hadn't. She didn't want to talk about them.

But he seemed to understand. "You think you'll be ready to ride with us next week?"

She nodded. "Prior to my accident, I spent a lot of time on horseback."

"There's going to be some long days," he said, leaning against the door frame.

Why was she suddenly nervous? He hadn't made a move in her direction. He hadn't even checked her out like he'd done in the barn. He was just standing there. In the doorway. Looking big. And handsome.

And male.

"When I'm at a show," she said, "I can be on my horse for hours at a time. Believe me, I'm used to it."

"Tell me something," he said, tipping his head to the

side. "How'd you afford all these shows? I've heard they can be expensive."

"I scrimp and save," she said. "As an amateur, I'm not allowed to have sponsors, so I pay for everything myself. Some years it's tough, but I love showing so much I'm willing to make sacrifices. My parents helped me out when they could. It was a terrific life..."

Before.

She didn't say the word out loud, but she didn't have to.

"You're really going to give all that up?"

She had to look away for a heartbeat. "I'm going to have to." There was no reason to hold on to her horse. Sooner or later—probably sooner based on the way her peripheral vision was shrinking—she'd be blind. Coaster was too sweet a horse to sit around. Plus, there'd been all those medical bills, and with his show record, he was worth a small fortune.

"I don't have a choice," she said through a throat thick with tears, because, damn she would miss him.

Come on, Sam. Buck up. At least you're alive.

"But it's okay," she said. "Coaster's young. He'll have a happy life in somebody else's barn."

"Is that your horse's name? Coaster?" he asked.

"Yeah. He's down in Texas right now, at a barn that specializes in quarter horses. My trainer thought we'd get more money for him there so he covered the cost of having him shipped down. My trainer will get a commission when Coaster sells."

And she'd be able to breathe a little easier. That's what she needed to focus on. Getting set for the future is all that mattered now, that and getting through life one day at a time.

"Hey," she said, having to inhale deeply to stop more

unwelcome tears from falling. She hated being such a crybaby. "I'd like to finish unpacking, if that's okay."

"Sure," he said, straightening away from the door. "But one more thing."

Another deep breath. That was better. She could feel her eyes drying up. "What's that?"

"Would you be willing to sign something?" he asked. "A nondisclosure form? If I draw one up?"

"Absolutely," she said. "I'll even promise to give you my firstborn son."

He stared at her, something flickering through his eyes. "That won't be necessary."

And then he was gone.

Sam sank onto the window sill.

SHE DIDN'T SEE CLINTON for the rest of the day. And when dinnertime came around, Gigi told her he went into town.

"Oh," Sam murmured, oddly disappointed.

"Come and sit down," Gigi said, motioning toward a table laden with food. "I'm known throughout the county for my famous meatloaf. Hopefully you'll like it. Go on. We can eat and chat."

They did exactly that, Sam growing more and more comfortable in the woman's presence. But though they stayed up late, Clint never returned. And when she got up in the morning, Gigi told her he was already out working. "He feeds the horses breakfast at five, and then he's off checking fences, or riding out to check stock, or hauling feed or doing something. Lots to do on a ranch this size."

"Surely he doesn't manage this place all by himself?"

"Good heavens, no," Gigi said as she set a plate of food in front of her. Eggs and bacon. "Our help comes in from town. They'll be here soon. Give it an hour and this place will be like Grand Central Station. But on the weekend, like yesterday, Clint keeps to himself."

"I see," Sam said, taking a forkful of food. "Oh, my gosh," she said, covering her mouth. "Those are the best eggs I've ever had."

"Heavy cream," Gigi said, standing at the stove and filling up her plate. When she turned back, Sam noticed she wore a white apron with a skull and crossbones. It covered most of the denim button-down shirt she wore and her darker blue jeans. "Just a dash," she said, sitting down across from her. "Makes them fluffier and sweeter. Clinton loves them."

Clinton.

Sam felt like a horse in a new pasture: on edge. Waiting for trouble to show up. Unable to settle down.

"So you think Clint'll be out all day?"

"I do," Gigi said, digging in. "You're free to roam around. Or use the phone. You mentioned last night that you wanted to check with the person who has your horse for sale in Texas."

"Coaster." Funny name for a horse, but it stemmed from his show name: Coasting in for Blues.

"You need a coaster?" Gigi asked, poised to get up from her chair and fetch her one.

"No," Sam said with a shake of her head. "That's my horse's name. Coaster."

"Oh." Gigi chuckled. "I see. Well, you can call after we finish breakfast."

Which she did. The horse broker who had him sounded pleased with his performance.

"We've had a lot of interest in him," the man said. "I wouldn't be surprised if we didn't have him sold by the end of the month."

Sold.

So soon.

She'd been hoping to get down there to see him before that. To ride him one last time….

"I see," she said.

"But I'll keep you posted."

"Thanks." She hung up the phone.

"What's the matter?" Gigi asked.

Sam shook her head. "Nothing." She pasted a grin on her face. "Good news, actually. There's been a lot of interest."

But Gigi didn't buy into the false cheer. Sam saw that immediately. "Are you sure you want to sell that animal?" she asked gently.

No. She didn't want to sell him, but she had to. "It's the best thing for him," she said softly.

"Yes, but is it the best thing for you?" Gigi asked, setting her fork down. "Sometimes, a horse is great therapy."

Sam nodded, refusing to cry today. She'd made enough of a boob of herself yesterday. "I think that's why I came here," she said. "Lots of horses to see." Though her savings account was running dangerously low thanks to her impromptu trip. She might not even have the money to get down to Texas to say goodbye.

"There certainly is that. And you're free to ride whichever one you choose."

But she had to ask Clint if she could do that, something she meant to do when she finally tracked him down in the barn. It was still dark outside—that was how early she'd gotten up. Roosters crowed in the distance. Cows moaned in complaint. Sam huddled into the thick, lavender-colored down jacket she'd brought along…just in case.

"Hey there," she said.

"Hey," he replied with barely a pause. He opened a

stall door and slipped inside. He was mucking out stalls, the scent of pine shavings filling the air. And, of course, he acted as if he hadn't just about scorched the pants right off her the last time they'd been together.

"Can I help?" she asked. "By the looks of it, you still have at least half the barn to go."

"No thanks," he said, shoving his straw cowboy hat down on his head. He didn't need it. Not this early in the morning. There was no sunlight—just bitter cold, something he'd bundled himself up against by wearing a denim jacket, jeans and boots—but she had a feeling it was a permanent part of his wardrobe.

"Help'll be here soon," he said. "They can finish up."

"But I'm here *now*," she answered, picking up a muck rake and heading inside the stall. Her short hair left the back of her neck exposed to the cold. "And I want to. I haven't done this in months."

Not since before the accident.

Her stomach turned. She clutched the end of the rake for support, holding it tight. Sometimes it physically hurt to think about her loss.

"You okay?" he asked.

"Of course," she said, although she was a little bit sore from her ride yesterday. But nothing too bad.

What am I doing here?

She should be at home, surrounded by the things she loved, mementos of her parents, photos, awards she'd won at horse shows. But, honestly, that's exactly why she'd left. She couldn't take it. Being there in her apartment. Alone. And so she'd gotten in her car and driven west before she'd known where she was going.

"You don't look okay," he said.

"I'm fine," she repeated, stabbing her fork into the pile of wood shavings at the horse's feet.

"Hey," he said, and suddenly there was a hand at her shoulder.

She froze. Reluctantly, slowly, she faced him, but she didn't meet his gaze.

"It might not seem like it, but I understand."

It took her a few second to get up the courage to look him in the eyes.

"If you need someone to talk to…" he began. How was it possible? How could she feel so immeasurably sad and yet aware of him at the same time.

"Thanks," she said.

He shuffled closer. She tensed.

"Sam," he said softly, as if test-driving the name, rolling it on his tongue to see how it tasted. He leaned down and Sam knew, she just knew, that he was about to kiss her.

Chapter Eight

"Mornin', Mr. McAlister."

They jumped apart.

"Didn't mean to startle you," the man added, studying Sam, who felt her cheeks heat. Silly reaction given nothing had happened.

Yet.

"Elliot," Clint said, nodding. "Nice to see you this morning."

The man nodded, the black leather hat he wore about the newest part of his attire, Samantha noticed. He had skin as worn and as wrinkled as an old quilt.

"Bones are gettin' a bit creakier," he said, "but I woke up this mornin'. Suppose that's not a bad thing."

"This is Sam," Clint said, rubbing a hand over his face.

She was still trying to stop herself from blushing.

"She's staying with us awhile," Clint added.

She was scanned as thoroughly as a can of goods at a checkout counter. "Pleasure to meet you, ma'am."

"And you," she said with what she hoped was a friendly smile, though it probably came out looking sickly because her face was still burning in reaction to their kiss…or *almost* kiss.

"What do you need me to do this mornin', boss?" Elliot asked.

"I was hoping you could move some hay around for me," Clint said. "I need some bales dropped out in pasture five, and some more hay brought into the barn."

"I'm on it," the man said, turning away.

"Isn't he too old to do that kind of work?" Sam asked, unable to stop herself. "I mean, he's got to be at least sixty."

"Seventy-five," Clint said. "All of his years out of doors have made him look older than he is but he can run circles around the other ranch hands."

"Oh." She looked away, ridiculously uncomfortable in his presence. "Cute horse," she said in an attempt to change the subject.

"No, he's not," Clint said, picking up a rake he'd managed to drop without her noticing. "He's a woolly mess. Losing his winter coat right now. Looks like a damn radiation victim."

Sam nearly smiled at his analogy. She crossed to the horse's side, stroked his shoulder. Hair poofed into the air around them. "He's not *that* bad," she lied. "Give me a curry and a body brush and I'll have him looking better in no time flat."

"Sounds like a deal to me," Clint said. "Brushes are in the tack box, his halter's hanging on the door."

"But don't you need help mucking out?"

"I already told you, I've got all the help I need arriving any second now."

As if to illustrate his point, someone else showed up. A kid. Well, all right. Maybe not a kid. Eighteen, nineteen years old. Battered brown cowboy hat, the color nearly matching his unkempt hair. Thick, denim jacket. Tattered pants. He looked like something the wind blew in.

"Mornin', boss," the guy greeted.

"Dean," Clint said from inside the stall, "Sam here was just inferring I don't have enough help. Would you please disabuse her of the notion?"

"Dis-a-what?" the kid asked, mouth hanging open. He had braces.

"Never mind," Clint said. "Hand us Pepper's halter. Miss Davies here's going to tidy him up."

"Hi, Dean," Sam said. "I'm Sam."

"Pleasure to meet you, ma'am."

Pleasure to meet you, ma'am. Gosh, she loved cowboys. On her way out west, everyone had been so polite. Apparently, people in the Midwest raised their children to respect their elders.

"Dean here lives on the next ranch over," Clint said, taking the halter from Dean's hands and slipping it over Pepper's head. "He works for us Monday through Friday."

Sam took the lead from Clint.

"And Sam here is going on the roundup with us," Clint said, opening the stall door.

"The *roundup?*" Dean asked, the front of his hat moving up he lifted his brows so high.

Sam clucked the horse forward, her feet bogged down by the thick bed of shavings in the stall.

What if Clint had tossed her down on those shavings and kissed her until she was dizzy with desire?

Sam!

"Yeah," Clint said, following her out. "Gigi thought she might like the ride."

The two men exchanged a look. "Terrific," he added, though Sam could tell he thought the idea anything but.

"Excuse me," she said heading for the cross-ties. She hadn't realized her presence on the roundup would cause trouble with anyone else but Clint. Obviously, women didn't usually go along.

She didn't know what to make of that as she brushed off Pepper. Clint and Dean worked on the barn while she tackled the somewhat messy job of brushing down a horse that was losing its winter coat. She ended up with more hair on her than on the horse…or so it felt like. Someone else arrived, and Clint sent the new guy out…to somewhere she didn't hear. Frankly, she didn't care. She was wondering if she'd made a mistake. If maybe she should gracefully bow out. What would Clint say if she did that? What would Gigi say?

"He looks pretty damn good," Clint said as she turned Pepper loose in his stall.

"Thanks." She unclipped the lead. Someone had fed the horses, the sweet smell of alfalfa filling the air. "If you want a horse's coat to shine, you have to brush him twice a day…sometimes more. You should see the halter horses on the quarter horse circuit. I swear you can see yourself in them, they're so shiny."

"Yeah, but none of our horses are going to show anytime soon. Just a roundup."

"I guess you're right."

She was tempted to tell him about her concerns as she left Pepper's stall. It wasn't like she was nervous, more like apprehensive. Though she had all the confidence in the world that she could ride the socks off most horses, she didn't know for certain. She'd been in an accident. And it'd been months since she was in a saddle for long stretches of time. She'd already suffered through one mishap….

"I know I asked you this before, but are you really sure you're going to be up to it?" he asked, reading her mind.

Tell him. Tell him now.

"Sure," she said with a lift of her chin. "It'll be good for me to get out."

"You think?"

She nodded firmly. "If you don't mind, I'd like to brush all the horses in the barn."

"Sure," he said. "Go ahead."

She nodded, but it was hell walking past him. She couldn't believe how much she wanted to stop, to turn to him, to take his hand. Instead she forced herself forward and peered into the next stall.

And froze.

"It's him," she said, admiring the dappled gray inside, the one with the blue eyes and the long mane. Unlike any breed she'd seen before. She'd wondered which stall he was in, or if he was kept in the barn. "Your horse. The one you were riding yesterday."

"That's him," he said, amused.

"He's one of your mustangs, isn't he?"

He didn't say anything, the silence growing to the point that Sam risked a peek up at him.

"You're afraid to answer that question, aren't you?" she asked. "Even after I promised to sign a nondisclosure, you're still worried I'll go off and blab it to the world."

She watched as he glanced at the horse, then back at her again. "I trust you'll keep your mouth shut. And, yes, he is one of our mustangs."

She smiled, a grin she was certain blinded him it was so bright. "How old is he?" she asked, opening the stall door and slipping inside. The horse lifted his head, studying her in the peculiar way horses had: ears pricked forward, pupils clearly focused on her, his thick forelock covering a portion of his face.

"Five."

"How do you know?"

"We microchip all our horses during our spring gatherings."

The spring gathering. The one she'd be going on in a couple of days.

If she didn't chicken out.

"He's beautiful."

Actual, living proof that the Baer Mountain Mustangs truly existed. How many times had her mom used a dappled gray gelding in her bedtime stories? To think that while Sam had been growing up, an ancestor of this horse—maybe even a dappled gelding like this one—had been running through the hills.

She moved forward, slowly, held out her hand. Would he pin his ears? Would he wrinkle his nose—a sure sign of equine displeasure?

His ears pricked forward.

"Hey there," she said softly. "What's your name?"

"Buttercup," Clint said.

She glanced at him sharply. "No, seriously. What is it?"

"Seriously. Buttercup," Clint said. And was that… could it be? Was that a *smile* on his face?

"No way," Sam said in reaction to both the smile *and* the horse's name. "I thought you were kidding when you told me that before."

"Gigi named him."

By now she could tell this was no wild mount who might bite her. She moved closer, lifting her palm to the horse's cheek, a favorite place for horses to be scratched—just above the cheekbone.

"You poor thing," she said, but the gelding didn't appear to mind his name. He leaned into her, clearly enjoying the attention. He even took a step forward. His feet rustled in the shavings, releasing pine scent into the air. "But you're gorgeous," she whispered.

Clint didn't say anything.

She glanced out the open stall door. Clint stood there, a curious expression on his face.

"Remember," he said, "you'll owe me your firstborn."

She'd like to give him a son.

That thought was so inappropriate and so out of the blue she found herself turning away, and blushing.

Jeesh. Was her feminine clock ticking or something?

But she couldn't deny that she wished he'd kissed her. There. She'd admitted it. She was seriously, wildly, unsuitably attracted to him. Here was someone who understood horses, someone who spoke her language. And who looked like he belonged on the cover of a western magazine to top it all off.

"Tell me about them," she said, still stroking the horse. "How did you get them?" she asked. "How have you cared for them all these years? Why do you care for them? What do you plan to do with them in the future?"

They were all questions she'd been dying to ask Gigi, but she hated to broach the subject. Gigi had been gracious enough to allow her to stay with them. She hadn't been comfortable grilling her.

"They were part of a land treaty in 1868," he said.

"A land treaty?"

He nodded, came forward and ran his hands through his horse's mane. She saw a world of tenderness in that touch, a gentleness in his eyes. He loved this animal, cared for him, soothed him when he was frightened with a comforting hand.

And maybe *that* was the root of her attraction. She needed someone. *Anyone,* to touch her like that. Lord knows, no one had held her since her parents died.

And could you sound any more desperate?

"My great-great-grandfather was a colonel in the

U.S. Army," he said. "Once the army decided to stop fighting the Sioux, he was in charge of peacetime efforts. William Baer knew he'd need some kind of common ground to help smooth negotiations. At his first meeting, he commented on the horses the Sioux rode. One thing led to another and in the end, the they were so grateful for all his efforts establishing peace, they gave him some of the horses he'd admired that first day."

"Wow," Sam said. "That's a truly remarkable tale."

"But that's not the end of the story." He absently scratched his horse near the withers. Buttercup lifted his head, his upper lip sticking out like an elephant's trunk.

"Once peace was established, the U.S. Army was under pressure to clear the western plains of wild mustangs. They were eating all the grass and leaving none for the cattle to graze on."

"What?"

"Yup. That movie *Hidalgo* was based on a true event. They were going to kill them all…or as many as they could get their hands on."

She gasped. "Could they do that?"

Buttercup was in ecstasy by now, leaning into Clint's hands. "They could do whatever they wanted," he said. "It was the United States government. The Sioux were helpless to stop it, and they knew it. My great-great-grandfather was outraged and so he took matters into his own hands. In the middle of the night, he and some of his Sioux friends stole the horses from where they'd been corralled. It was a daring thing to do. Two hundred head of horses right out from beneath the U.S. Army's nose."

"Obviously, he succeeded."

"Yup. No one could ever prove it was him. But the Sioux knew. Horses were sacred to them. So they gave him some of the land ceded to them in the Treaty of Fort Laramie—the bulk of what we now own—and entrusted him with preserving their precious horses."

"The Baer Mountain Mustangs."

Clint nodded, patting the horse. Buttercup lowered his head in disappointment. "We've taken great care to maintain the bloodline, but by doing so they're not really wild mustangs anymore. You'll see more of that when you ride out with us. There's three different herds. We geld the colts and mix and match the fillies with the other herds. That way there's no inbreeding and we're able to protect their unique heritage."

And she would be one of the few people who would ever get to see them. "How have you managed to keep this a secret for so long?"

He shrugged, fiddled with his horse's mane. "The Sioux know, of course. We still trade with them from time to time. It's a good way to introduce new blood into the herd. There've been other people who've guessed over the years. Rumors. Some of our ranch hands have come and gone, a few of them have let the secret out. But we've always denied it. Until you."

"Until me," she repeated.

"Yeah," he said, scratching his chin. "Although to be honest, I'm still not convinced that was such a smart idea."

"But I'll never tell anyone," she said, suddenly terrified he wouldn't let her see the horses. "I promise the minute you put that nondisclosure agreement in front of me, I'll sign it."

"No."

"No?" She felt as if she was losing her parents all over again.

"I can think of only one way to keep you quiet."

And suddenly her heart rate tripled. There was a look in his eyes....

"And what's that?" she asked.

"I'm gonna have to go to bed with you."

Chapter Nine

"Go to bed with me," Samantha Davies squeaked.

Clint almost laughed at the look on her face. If he didn't know for a fact that she was attracted to him, he'd have been insulted. But he remembered only too well how close he'd come to kissing her earlier—and how much she'd wanted him to do it, too. He could see it in her eyes.

"Come on," he teased. "It won't be that bad. One night in my bed in exchange for seeing the horses."

"You're crazy."

"Am I?" he asked, stepping toward her.

She started to back away.

Stop it, Clint. You're going to scare her.

But he couldn't seem to stop himself. And to be honest, there was a part of him that wanted to see how far she'd go. To see how badly she wanted him. Or how badly she wanted to see his mustangs. And they were *his* horses, not that Sam knew that. Grandma Gigi might be a Baer, but the ranch and all its belongings had been deeded to him after his grandfather's death. It would have gone to his mother if she'd still been alive, but sadly, that hadn't been the case, although in hindsight Clint was convinced Gigi had deeded the place to him as a way of keeping him busy after his grandfather's death. He'd loved Grandpa Baer as much as Gigi had.

"Look," she said, holding out a hand, "I want to see your horses, I'm not going to lie. It means a lot to me. But I'm not going to sleep with you just so I can go out on some extended trail ride."

"A trail ride?" he asked. He had her cornered now. There was no place to go except out of the stall, but he noticed she didn't make a dash for it. No. She pressed her back against the oak panels and stared up at him, her chest rising and falling.

It turned him on.

Her hair was so short that it left the back of her neck exposed. He'd been longing to kiss those fine hairs at the nape of her neck ever since he'd first spotted her standing there in the barn, all bundled up in her purple jacket, cheeks pink from cold.

"Well, okay. A roundup. But frankly it's nothing more than a trail ride when you come right down to it."

"Lady, what we'll be doing will be a lot more than riding the trails."

"I know," she said. "But that's beside the point. I'm not sleeping with you."

"No?" he asked, so close to her now that he could feel heat radiating off her body. The sun had started to come up, warm light filtering through the barn. It turned her green eyes the color of the hay that dotted the stall floor.

"No," she said firmly.

"Funny," he said softly, "I could have sworn you wanted me to kiss you earlier."

She lifted her chin.

You're going too far.

But he couldn't stop. She was like a newborn

foal—skittish and standoffish, but something he was tempted to tame.

"*You* wanted to kiss *me*," she corrected.

"Actually," he said softly, giving in to the urge to touch her, his fingers making contact with the side of her neck, "I think you're right."

He *was* going to kiss her. No sense in denying it. He was going to kiss her and damn the consequences.

"Clint," she murmured, and was that a sigh of longing, or a huff of warning? Didn't matter. She didn't dart away.

She wanted him.

"Pucker up, woman."

"Excuse—"

He sucked the rest of her words right out of her mouth. He didn't mean to. He just meant to give her a little peck on the lips. But the moment he tasted her, the instant his lips made contact with hers, he was lost.

Damn.

She tasted like Gigi's coffee. And something else. Something he didn't recognize at first.

Cinnamon.

It clung to her lips. She pressed against him and he felt his whole body jerk in response. He couldn't seem to make himself pull back and so he pushed her against the wall instead, tipped his head to the side and branded her with his lips.

Her hands lifted to his chest, slipped beneath his jacket against his flesh, her fingers exploring every ridge of his chest, sliding upward until she found his shoulders.

He pulled his head away, he'd had to—he needed to breathe. But as soon as his mouth left hers, he wanted to dive back for more. She was like a cool lake on a hot, summer day. All he wanted was to keep plunging beneath the surface...plunging and plunging and plunging.

And so he angled his head the opposite direction and kissed her again. His hands found the slit in her jacket, her warmth startling him. She arched into him.

"Crap," he muttered, tossing his head back and sucking in yet another breath. "This is crazy."

His hand was near the curve of her breast and so he stroked her side with his thumb and found the soft edge near the bottom. When he glanced down, her eyes were shielded by her lashes, her lips red from his kiss.

He wanted her.

Wanted her like he hadn't wanted a woman in a long, long time…since Julia. That was enough to make him let her go.

"I think," he said, lifting his hand to the back of his neck and shaking his head, "that I'm going to have to find another way to keep you quiet."

SHE LEFT THE BARN. SHE KNEW it was cowardly, but she needed some space between her and Clint.

"There you are!" Gigi said when she entered the house.

Sam drew up short, almost as if Gigi could see into her head. God, were her lips red? Could Gigi tell what had just happened by the blush on her cheeks. Were her clothes rumpled?

"Your horse broker called back, said he's headed off to a show and not to panic if he doesn't immediately return your calls."

Sam nodded, knowing if she didn't, Gigi would be suspicious. "Thanks," she said, swiping at a lock of hair in her face, but when she closed the front door she almost leaned against it.

"You okay?" Gigi asked.

"Fine," she said. "I'm just a little tired."

Gigi stepped toward her, suddenly all business. "Are

you sleeping okay? I know sometimes after an accident like yours…"

After Sam had woken up in the hospital, all she'd wanted to do was rest. But then her injuries had healed and sleep had become the enemy. She would dream about the first terrifying lurch of the car's backend. About screams. About someone crying in pain—her mom, or maybe herself. The sound of a chainsaw. So, yes, she *was* tired. Always tired.

"Sam?"

Sam jerked, brought back to earth by the sound of Gigi's voice. "I'm okay," she said. "Really. It's just cold outside. My mouth needs to defrost."

But Gigi didn't miss a thing. The older woman scanned her face thoroughly. "I see," she said, Sam was afraid she *saw* far too much.

"I'm going up to my room."

"I'm heading into town later if you want to join me," Gigi said.

"That'd be great." It might be a smart idea to get away.

But for the next few hours Sam kept replaying what had happened in the barn. Had she been too forward? Should she have allowed him to get so close? Did he think she was easy because she'd let him kiss her?

What the hell had she been thinking?

That was the question that kept repeating itself over and over again. Even as Sam was charmed by Williams, Montana—named after Clint's great-great-grandfather, she'd learned—she'd been distracted. It was a lovely day, though, and when she returned her embarrassment had faded. Her only fear was that Clint would regret what had happened. Except he was nowhere to be found.

"Why don't you saddle up one of the horses in the barn and ride?" Gigi asked. "Unless you're too sore."

"No. I'm fine," Sam said. Remarkably, she felt very few aches.

"Excellent. You should probably start building your stamina for the roundup. We leave two days from now."

Gigi had a point. And so Sam busied herself with the familiar task of grooming the little palomino mare Gigi had recommended. Coaster would be cared for by someone else, soon. Someone else would get to feed him carrots or his favorite oatmeal treats.

"You look sad."

Sam jumped because, of course, it was Clint.

"Hi," she said, her heart suddenly beating so hard and fast it made her breathless.

"What were you thinking?"

She hadn't seen him approach or heard him, although he was leading a horse into the barn. Buttercup, she realized.

"Nothing," she said, going back to grooming the palomino whose name she didn't know. "Just thinking," she added, trying to sound dismissive and failing terribly. It was horrible, this attraction she felt. All right, maybe not horrible. More like startling. She couldn't come within two feet of the guy without blushing like a teenager.

"You going riding?"

She nodded.

"Great. I'll go with you."

That caused her to turn toward him. "Don't you have work to do?"

He shook his head. "I'm free for the next hour. Just finished fixing that fence post I was working on yesterday. I was going to ride out and open the gate so the cows can graze in there now. You could ride with me."

Ride with him.

"Okay," she said slowly. "Sure. I'll keep you company."

He smiled. "Good. Let me tie up Buttercup here and I'll tell you what tack to use on Inca."

"Is that her name?"

He nodded.

"Is she a mustang?" she asked, watching as he put Buttercup on cross-ties near the end of the barn.

"No. She's a quarter horse. We don't break a lot of the mustangs. They can be damn stubborn to work with. Too many decades of being undomesticated."

"But they're used to you going up to them, right?" she said. "I mean, you said you microchip them. I assume that means you interact with them on a regular basis."

He motioned for her to follow him into the tack room, which she did, though it caused her heart palpitations. Would he kiss her there? What if he tried?

He didn't.

"Use this bridle here," he said, lightly touching a curb bit hanging on a rack. He went and picked up the same saddle she'd used yesterday, or so it seemed. "And, yeah, we interact with the horses regularly. But we rarely do anything more than sort 'em out, give them their yearly vaccines, that sort of thing. So you couldn't really say they're 'handled.'"

"How did you end up with Buttercup?" she asked, following him out of the tack room.

"He was an orphan foal. None of the mares would adopt him and so we had to bring him in. But you can clearly see how different he looks from, say, the quarter horses. The blue eyes are common in our mustangs. The refined heads, too. We think that comes from their Spanish blood."

"Are they mostly grays?" she asked, as he threw a saddle blanket on Inca's back and then the saddle.

"No. Most are paints, but we have a few Appaloosas, too, mixed in with bays and sorrels."

She could stand there all day and listen to him talk about his horses. She felt her spirits lift. She'd done the right thing by coming here. There might be this "thing" between her and Clint, but she could deal with that. And, really, if it went any further, would that be bad? Why not jump into bed with a handsome cowboy? What was wrong with that?

He finished what he was doing, turned to her. "I'll let you bridle her yourself."

"Not a problem," she said, taking the leather headstall from him.

He went and unclipped his own horse. Sam felt her heart tick faster for an altogether different reason. She would get to ride again. In Montana's wide-open spaces. Could life get any better?

It might if that life included a cowboy named Clint.

Chapter Ten

"You look good for someone who's only ever ridden in an English saddle," Clint found himself saying, the two of them having left the homestead behind. They were out past the arena now, approaching one of the many pastures that surrounded the homestead. Barbwire fence stretched for miles in both directions.

"Thanks," she said, her smile as white as the snow on top of the mountains. "You look good, too."

And there it was again, the glint in her eyes that made them sparkle and made him think, damn, I wish we weren't on horseback so I could push her up against another stall wall.

"I doubt it," he said sheepishly. "I've been out trying to fix that damn fence all morning. Took me forever to get the post sunk in deep enough, and then longer still to restring the wire better than I did yesterday. That was just a temporary fix."

Buttercup tossed his head when they reached the pasture gate, and Clint opened it from the back of his horse.

"Impressive," she said when he moved his horse back so she could step through. "You could compete on the quarter horse circuit, too, in the trail riding class."

He reversed his horse again so he could close the gate. "I'm no fancy show rider."

"Neither am I," she said, stopping so he could catch up. "The outfits we wear might look expensive, but I'm just an average girl from a middle-class family who's saved her money to fund her habit—showing horses."

Her hair might be short, but the wind still played with it. Clint would never forget the sight of her in the saddle, her short brown hair blowing around her face, her green eyes glowing, the backdrop of mountains and pasture.

"I've heard it costs a lot of money."

"It does," she said. "Some people like to ski, or boat or fish. Those are expensive hobbies, too. Mine just involves a four-legged animal."

"Yeah, but you can put your fishing poles in a garage, you can't do that with a horse."

"True," she said, pushing her bangs away from her eyes. "Training and board are expensive. I gave up horses for a while to go to college and get a degree. I did it to make a decent living…so I could afford to show my horse. In between vet bills, shoeing and all the other incidental charges, it can be pricey on a monthly basis. Needless to say, I don't have a whole lot of money in my savings account."

"So you're selling your horse," he said, kicking Buttercup forward so the two of them were even.

"Yeah."

"Is that what made you so sad earlier?"

She glanced at him sharply. "Sheesh, you have the most amazing way of doing that."

"Doing what?"

"Reading my mind. You seem to know exactly what I'm thinking."

"I'm psychic," he said.

"No, you're not. You're just good at reading people. It comes with working with horses, I've noticed. You mind if we trot."

"No," he said. "I don't mind if we *jog*."

That made her laugh, which lifted Clint's own spirits far more than it should.

"Well?" he asked, squeezing his horse into the requested gate. "Is it?"

"Is it what?" she asked in an obvious attempt at being evasive."

"Is it selling your horse that made you sad?"

She didn't answer for a while, but that was okay with Clint. He enjoyed the sounds of nature, of the rhythmic jingle of his spurs as Buttercup jogged along. The sound of the prairie birds in the distance. The soft thuds of hooves in the grass.

"It is," she admitted at last. Clint glanced over at her. She had a perfect profile. Pert nose. Tiny chin. Generous mouth. That mouth was pressed into a flat line, one that conveyed the sadness she fought so hard to hide.

He pulled his gelding up. She followed suit. "What is it?" she asked.

"Have you lost everything, Samantha?"

She blinked, shielding her eyes from his view, but not before he read what was in them.

"You mentioned medical bills before. And that you're going to have to sell your horse. You don't have a job. I didn't see what you unpacked from the car, but Gigi said it looked like everything you owned."

She shook her head. "No, I haven't lost everything."

He finished the sentence for her. "Yet."

"Hopefully not ever," she said. "Coaster is worth twenty thousand at least, probably more. That'll cover a large portion of my medical bills, and hopefully leave me enough to pay the rest of my bills."

"And if you don't sell him?"

She shrugged. "I might have to move. Find a new place to live. Another job. But I will definitely have to sell Coaster. My job as a geologist doesn't pay enough for me to catch up."

He nodded and decided to change the subject. She looked even more sad than when she'd been in the barn. "Why'd you go into geology?"

She shrugged. "I'd heard there were always jobs in the oil industry. Honestly, I thought it'd be easy to graduate, find a job in Texas, maybe buy a ranch later on."

"Why Texas?"

"Are you kidding?" she asked. "That's the heart of quarter horse country."

He rolled his eyes. "Why am I not surprised?"

"But I couldn't find a job there. Best offer came out of Wilmington, Delaware, working for a chemical company. They send me out to survey property. A lot of the chemicals used in their products are petroleum based."

"Sounds like a great job."

"It was."

"So?" he asked. "What happened?"

She shrugged again.

"You said the other day you had problems. What kind of problems?"

"Just some physical limitations."

"Such as."

She finally looked him straight in the eye. "An injury to my brain. It's caused some…" She searched for the word. "Complications. To my body. I'm technically disabled now, but I manage to get around okay."

He wanted to ask her what kind of complications, but

he could tell she was hesitant to talk about it. And when it came down to it, who was he to ask? They barely knew each other.

"So, you won't be able to find another job?"

She shook her head. "Not for a long time."

"And now you're forced to sell your horse."

She nodded, sucking her lower lip between her teeth. "It's what I have to do," she said. "I don't have a choice."

He had to turn away. Looking at her, seeing the sadness in her eyes, it did things to him. What if he had to leave the Baer Mountain Ranch? He knew that would never happen, but what if?

"You've had some rotten luck," he finally said.

"E-yup. But, hey, at least I'm alive."

Unlike her parents. God, he couldn't imagine. Waking up and finding out your mom and dad were dead, and then discovering you were disabled and would have to quit your job. Maybe move, sell your horse....

"Ready to run?" He wanted—needed—to put a smile on her face.

"Sure. I think I can manage that."

He didn't even have time to cram his hat more firmly on his head.

She kicked Inca and off she went. Clint held Buttercup back for an instant—much to the horse's disgust—just so he could admire her style. Man, she could ride. She leaned forward, legs quiet against her horse's side, as if she were a part of her horse.

"Go," he told Buttercup.

And his horse didn't need to be told twice.

SHE'D ALMOST TOLD HIM. Almost told him she was going blind.

Once again, Sam shut her eyes, imagining what it

would be like. Inca thundered beneath her, her hooves like jungle drums. Ba-da-dump, ba-da-dump, ba-da-dump. Wind poked at Sam's eyes, causing them to tear up. Or were those tears from something else?

Not again. She would *not* cry.

She opened her eyes. The grass was nothing but a blur beneath her. Ahead was open pasture. Behind her, the Baer Mountains.

For a second her vision blurred and panic took her breath away. She sucked in a breath, quickly wiping her eyes. Better.

"Sam!" Clint called.

She shook her head. But Buttercup was born to run. He had the taut athleticism of an animal whose ancestors had outmaneuvered prey for hundreds of years. With every stride Clint came closer. She leaned forward, tried to urge her horse faster. But it was no use. Clint caught her.

"Sam," he repeated. "Stop."

She didn't want to. She wanted to keep on running… and running…maybe one day outdistancing her pain.

She pulled up out of kindness to Inca. Pastures were tricky. All it would take was a tiny hole or a thick patch of grass…something that would tangle in her legs or hooves and bring them down.

"Whoa," she said softly, leaning back. But she didn't dash her tears away quickly enough.

"You're crying," he said when he had Buttercup stopped.

"The wind in my eyes."

"Yes, you are," he said, dismounting.

Her mare shook her head, as if chastising her for running her so fast. "I'm okay," she said. "Really."

But he ignored her, dropping his reins and crossing to her. "Get down."

"Why?"

"Because you need to let it out."

"No, I don't," she said, attempting, and failing, at sounding outraged.

"Sam," he said gently. "Get down. You're like a race horse, ready to explode out of the gate."

She wiped her eyes again because, damn it, another tear had managed to escape. "Only you would use a horse analogy," she said, slipping out of the saddle. She sounded like Alvin the chipmunk her nose was so clogged.

She was shaking now, trying so damn hard not to lose control. Breathe in. Breathe out.

But she couldn't do it. She could feel her control crumbling like the ancient hills behind her.

She couldn't do it anymore. She couldn't be strong. She wanted her mom. And her dad. She wanted her life back.

She wanted *not* to go blind.

"I don't think. I just don't know—"

And then she was in his arms, sobbing, crying like she'd never cried before.

Chapter Eleven

Clint held her. "I'm sorry," he said. "So damn sorry."

"'Sokay," he heard Sam slur. "'S not your fault."

He rested his head against the top of her short-cropped hair. She fit him so perfectly. Like two pieces of a jigsaw, her curves fitting into his concaves as if they'd been cut apart at birth. "I still ache for you."

She sucked in a breath, clinging to him as if she was afraid she'd sink below the surface if she didn't hold on.

"Thank you," she said a long while later.

He'd been rocking her, slowly, gently. "You're paying my dry cleaning bill," he said.

"Dry cleaning bill," she repeated, drawing back and wiping at her eyes. Other women would look hideous after such a crying jag. Not Sam. "You look like you need a blow-dryer."

"Sorry. No blow-dryers in my saddle pack."

She smiled slightly. Progress.

"You've been so kind to me."

He gave her one last hug before setting her away from him. Frankly, he had to retreat because he was starting to feel something for her. "Yeah, well, don't tell anyone," he said. "You'll ruin my reputation as a surly old cowboy."

"You're not old," she said, sniffing. "And you're certainly not surly."

"Come on," he said, turning to see where his horse had run off to. Always made him laugh when he watched those old cowboy movies, the horses never moving once the reins had been dropped. It was a rare horse, indeed, that wouldn't wander, even with grass nearby. Sure enough, both horses were at least twenty paces away. "Let's get on before they head back to the barn."

But before he'd taken a step he heard her say, "Clint."

He faced her again, reluctantly.

"I realize you didn't want me here...not at first," she said. "But I just wanted to say how much I appreciate you and your grandmother's generosity. You two are strangers to me, but you've treated me like family." Her breath sounded jagged. "I needed that right now."

That's why he hadn't given in to the urge to kiss her, though it nearly killed him. But the timing was all wrong. It might never be right.

He moved away, fetched her horse for her and then held the reins while she mounted.

"Which way?" she asked.

"WHERE'D YOU TWO RIDE OFF TO?" Gigi asked him later that night.

They'd just finished dinner, Samantha having already gone up to her room for the night. Clint knew his grandmother was brimming with questions. She must have sensed Sam's subdued mood, and noticed that he couldn't keep his eyes off Sam.

"We rode out to open the south gate," he said. "After I fixed that fence line."

Gigi got up, began to clear plates. Clint got up to help her.

"She looked like she'd been crying."

Now, how had she guessed? "She broke down while we were out riding."

"Broke down?" Gigi asked.

Clint batted Gigi's hands away from the dishes, butting her out of the way. "Let me do that."

"By all means," she said, motioning for him to continue.

"Did she tell you she's disabled?" he asked.

"Disabled how?"

He shook his head, put one of the dirty plates under the warm stream of water. Sam's dishes were already in the sink—food untouched.

"Don't know," he said. "Didn't ask."

"She looks fine."

"Yeah," he said. "But then we started talking about her having to quit her job, having to sell her horse—"

"Poor dear."

"She's really had a tough time of it."

"She sure has," Gigi said, crossing her arms in front of her. "So what are we going to do about it?"

"We aren't going to do anything but take her up to see our horses," he said, opening the dishwasher and setting the clean plate inside.

"Clinton, that girl is all alone, without a friend in the world."

"It's none of our business," he said, picking up another plate.

She huffed. "Of course it's our business. She's a guest in our house, and let me tell you, the whole time she's been here I haven't heard her cell phone ring once. And she doesn't call anyone. Heck, she hasn't even asked if we have Internet."

"She's probably afraid to impose," he said.

"You're right. She probably is. She's not like Julia."

The plate slipped out of his hands and landed with a clatter against the stainless steel.

"Did it break?" she asked, peering into the sink.

"No," he said. "But if it had, it would have been your fault. Why'd you have to go and mention *her?*"

"Because you almost married her. Fortunately, you woke up in time, but not before you were hurt. I'm worried you might be afraid to put your hat in the arena one more time."

"Meaning you don't mind me dating Samantha Davies, but you don't want me sleeping with her," he said, taking Gigi's plate from the pile. Hopefully he wouldn't drop this one.

"I'll have none of that kind of talk in here."

"Why not?" he asked. "You were the one who told me to keep my paws off of her."

"Because I thought all you wanted was sex. Now I'm not so certain."

"What made you change your mind?"

"You took her out on a trail ride."

He set Gigi's plate down, shut off the water. "What does taking her on a trail ride have to do with the price of tea in China?"

Gigi studied him intently. "You don't mix business with pleasure. The last time you did that was with—"

"Julia," he finished for her.

"Yes."

"And look where that got me."

"Sam's different."

"Sam's got a whole lot more on her mind than me."

"Have you kissed her?"

He'd been in the middle of scraping off Sam's plate, but the damn thing almost slipped from his grasp, too.

"You *have,* haven't you?"

"No comment," he grumbled.

"Just be careful, Clint. She's fragile right now."

"You don't know her well enough to say that."

"Yes, I do. I know her heart. And it's a good one. Unlike—"

Julia's. He didn't say the name. Didn't need to.

"I just want you to be careful. What that girl needs right now is a shoulder to cry on."

"Believe me, she had one this afternoon."

"Good. And some kindness, too. We've been blessed, you and I. Yes, we've had more than our fair share of tragedies, but we've had each other, this ranch, friends…. Sam has no one."

And nothing to look forward to, either. That seemed a shame. A damn shame.

"I'll give her some space, if that's what you want."

"Take things slow with her. Shower her with love."

"Love?"

"You know what I mean."

No, he didn't. "You want me to sleep with her now?"

"That wasn't what I was inferring at all," his grandmother spat.

"Then what did you mean?"

"Do something nice for her. The poor dear is in desperate need of a random act of kindness."

Yeah, she was. He got the impression Sam had never had a helping hand. Her parents had been there for her, but purely as emotional support. She'd put herself through school. Supported her own riding career. Lived on her own.

"Let me think what I can do."

THE NEXT MORNING HE WAS no closer to figuring out what "random act of kindness" would be appropriate for someone they barely knew. He got dressed in his clean denim shirt and jeans, half expecting to bump into Sam. Yesterday, she'd seemed anxious to help, but today she was nowhere in sight. He went outside to feed the horses, but when he came back in for breakfast, she still wasn't around.

Gigi looked worried. "I brought her breakfast earlier. She thanked me, but claimed she wasn't hungry."

Clint kissed the top of Gigi's head. "I'll go check on her."

He went to her room, lifting his hat and running a hand through his hair before softly knocking. "You there?" he asked.

She didn't respond.

Had she gone back to sleep? He knocked again, louder. Still no answer.

Crap, what if...she'd *killed* herself?

He opened the door. She gasped, turning away from the window, clutching the robe she was wearing tightly around her. "What the hell?"

"Sorry," he said. "When you didn't answer, I...got worried."

"Well, as you can see, I'm fine," she said. The morning light outlined her hair and set it aglow.

He stepped into the room.

"What are you doing?"

"I'm trying to figure out what's wrong. Last night, at dinner, you seemed fine. Maybe light on appetite, but fine."

She shook her head. "Nothing's wrong. I just didn't sleep well, is all."

"No," he said. "You're not fine. Anyone who cried as hard as you did yesterday is definitely *not* fine."

"That's just it," she said. "I shouldn't have lost it like

I did. I barely know you guys, yet all I've done is blubber on your shoulder ever since I've come here."

He moved closer to her, and though he knew he shouldn't, he couldn't help but notice how sexy her legs were.

What a caveman you are, Clint.

"What happened?" he asked.

"What do you mean, what happened?" she asked. "Nothing's happened."

"Bull," he said. "I can tell something's set you off."

She shook her head.

"What happened?" He closed the distance between them.

She looked down at the floor, and Clint could tell she wanted to tell him.

"Sam," he said gently, lifting her chin, "I told you yesterday, if you need a shoulder…"

She sucked in a breath, her pupils dilating. "Yeah, but you were just being kind," she said softly.

"I sincerely want to help. Tell me. What happened?"

Chapter Twelve

As if from a distance, Sam heard herself say, "Someone bought my horse this morning. I got a very early call. They bought him sight unseen. He's being shipped out after the wire transfer clears the bank."

Clint studied her for a moment, concern written on his face. Finally, he pulled her into his arms, murmuring, "Aww, Sam. I'm sorry."

She'd grown numb. Gigi and Clint were nice people. She had to stop burdening them with her troubles.

"I'm okay," she said, stiff in his arms, but not because she was afraid she might cry. She was naked under her robe. And Clint…his body was hard and hot and she was starting to tingle in places….

"Are you sure you're okay?" he asked, drawing back.

"Yeah," she said. "I just can't…I mean, I know it's for the best, but it still hurts. I've had Coaster since he was a baby. Raised him. Trained him. Now he's going to someone else's barn, and with my life the way it is…"

"You might never see him again," he said, his voice full of understanding.

She stepped away from him.

"It was a great offer," she said, running a hand

through her short hair. "Money I couldn't refuse. Twenty thousand. So I gave the go-ahead."

"Wow," he said. "Isn't that great news?"

No. "Yeah," she said.

And for a moment she let herself be angry. What the hell kind of dark cloud had she fallen under to lose her parents, her job, her horse, and soon, her vision?

"Look," she said, pulling the robe around her, "thanks for caring enough to check on me. I appreciate that. But I'll be fine."

She expected him to nod. For sure she expected him to leave. Instead he removed his hat, ran a hand through his hair.

"I know it's probably not going to be the same," he said, "but we have a boatload of horses around here. If you'd like, I'll give you one."

She couldn't speak for a heartbeat. "You'll give me one?"

"Sure," he said. "Why not. Like I said, horses are something we have a lot of."

She shook her head. "You don't have to do that. Really. I'll get over losing Coaster." Sooner or later.

He didn't look convinced.

"I mean it," she said, grabbing his arm and leading him to the door. "I'm fine. But I plan on staying out of everyone's hair today so don't be worried if you don't see me. I promise not to kill myself."

"I never thought you were going to kill yourself," he said, dragging his heels.

But honestly, every time she touched him—no matter how fragile her emotional state—she didn't want to let him go. It was frightening how badly she wanted him.

"You thought something bad had happened. I could see it in your eyes."

He didn't say anything, and she knew she shouldn't do it…knew it was a bad idea, but she couldn't seem to stop from reaching up on tiptoe and kissing him on the cheek. "You're the sweetest man I've ever met," she admitted, pulling back before she did something even more crazy like undo her robe and place his hand against her breast.

But when she stepped away, he didn't let her go. "You wouldn't think I was sweet if you knew what I was thinking right now."

She froze.

"If you had any idea how much I want to part that robe of yours, to see if you're wearing anything beneath it."

Her mouth dropped open. *Don't be silly. Of course I'm wearing something beneath this. What kind of girl do you think I am?* "I'm not."

His eyes flashed, and Sam recognized that she'd crossed a line, one that put the ball in his court.

He stepped back. Sam tried not to let her shoulders slump.

He closed the door.

Sam felt her body throb to life.

He pulled her to him, and the carnal way he kissed her told Sam all she needed to know. This would be no slow seduction.

And then she stopped thinking.

His tongue seared her mouth. She arched into him, offering herself, begging him without words that she wanted him to part her robe, to put his hand on her, touch her….

He did exactly that.

She groaned, closing her eyes as his hand found her naked breast. His thumb and forefinger lightly stroked her, and then gently—ever so softly—squeezed her. She almost sagged to the ground the sensation was so exquisite. When he pulled his lips away, Sam's eyes opened in disappointment.

He was bending, his mouth moving to the tip of her nipple and—oh, dear—sucking it. "Clint," she moaned.

Somehow she was moving backward, toward the bed, Sam sinking onto it while Clint continued to lick and then nip and then gently bite. And she was pressing herself against him, lifting her hips off the bed because it'd been so long...so long since she'd been with a man.

His hand glided downward. She knew where that hand was headed, her body erupting in anticipation of it touching her. He paused for a second at her hips. She tipped toward him in such a way that he wouldn't be able to mistake what she wanted him to do. Stroke her. There.

He did.

Softly at first, then with more and more pressure. She pushed against him, trying to encourage him without words to delve deeper. He did as asked.

She would remember this, she thought. Remember what it felt like. Smelled like. Looked like. That most of all. So when his lips left her breasts to follow the same path as his hand, she watched him, reached out and touched his hair. But the lower he moved, the harder it became to keep her eyes open. It felt so good. She wanted to lean back and savor every sensation. He kissed her side, lingering there for a few breaths, tickling her with razor stubble, and then he shifted, licked her left hip.

"Clint," she said softly, bright flashes of light exploding behind her eyes.

When he nipped her, she groaned, which prompted him to suckle her for a moment, his teeth beginning to blaze a path toward her center and she knew he was going to put his mouth there. Electricity danced down her veins and all the way to her toes. Sam was unable to breathe as she waited for him to finally arrive. She opened her eyes, glanced down. He stared up at her, his stunning blue eyes dark with desire. And then she saw his head begin to lower and Sam hovered on the brink of an orgasm just watching him there, knowing he was about to taste her.

Heat stroked her center.

She cried out, arched back.

He licked her again.

Yes!

She parted for him, allowed him complete access because she wanted this. Oh, how she wanted this. She hadn't been this turned on since, well, since forever.

He kept his mouth anchored there, Sam's hips lifting toward him, urging him on. She knew she was going to lose control, thought for an instant that she should pull him up, unzip his pants, guide him to her.

A spasm rocked her body, one so intense, so delicious she came off the bed. She opened her eyes, watched his blond head down there, saw her abdomen spasm as he brought her to the ultimate pinnacle of pleasure.

"Clint." She sighed, so grateful, so moved by his commitment, that she reached out and gently stroked his head. "Your turn."

He kissed her inner thigh, latched his lips onto her there. "Not yet."

"Please?"

"Let's not rush this," he said, moving up her body, his hand lingering at her side.

She wasn't inexperienced in these matters. She could seduce *him* as quickly as he'd seduced *her.* But for now she let him draw things out.

"Sam?" Gigi called.

They pulled apart. Sam reached down and swung the bedspread around her.

"You there?" Gigi called again through the door, tapping lightly.

"I'm here," Sam said, scrambling for the covers.

"You okay?" Gigi asked.

She nearly laughed.

Was she okay?

Geez. She'd never been better. "I'm fine," she said. "Just in bed."

"You seen Clint?"

Sam and Clint exchanged glances. Sam had to cover her mouth with her hand to keep herself from laughing. Clint silently shushed her. "I saw him earlier," she called.

Silence.

Sam's cheeks flamed. She had a feeling Gigi knew exactly where Clint was.

"Well, all right," she said through the closed doors. "If you need anything, just call. These walls are paper-thin."

At that, Sam leaned her head back and started to laugh silently.

These walls are paper-thin.

In other words, if Clint's in there, you two better be quiet.

"I should go," Clint said a beat later.

"Clint, no," she said. "We can keep things down."

He shook his head, his blue eyes all but sparkling. "You think so?"

"Well, maybe not."

"As much as I hate to leave," he said, "knowing my grandmother is on the other side of the wall…. Besides, I've got a boatload of work to do today. Got to get ready for the roundup tomorrow."

She smiled.

He leaned over her, kissed her tenderly. Sam's body came alive again when she tasted herself on his lips. This man turned her on like nobody else.

"I'll see you later," he said.

"Yes." She *would* see him. She would see him for as long as God gave her the eyes to do so.

She only hoped that would be for a long time to come.

Chapter Thirteen

Sam woke up the next morning feeling more relaxed than she had in a long, long time. She'd had a terrific day yesterday, although when she'd gone to bed last night she'd lain awake hoping Clint would come to her room. He hadn't and so she'd reluctantly gone to sleep. But today was a new day.

And she could still see.

The embolism—that horrible *E* word that she refused to say out loud because then it would make it real—had not worsened.

She had a central retinal occlusion brought on by a brain embolism, in other words, a really large blood clot that was cutting off her retina's blood supply. But despite her fears, she probably wouldn't go suddenly blind. More likely the pressure would increase to the point that slowly, inevitably, she'd lose her sight. She'd already experienced steady shrinking of her peripheral vision. That would only continue.

But she wouldn't think about that now. Right now what she wanted to think about was Clint.

She nestled her head into her pillow. He'd come to her room yesterday and made her moan his name and convulse with pleasure. Hopefully, he would do it again. Tonight. Someplace private.

She got up and dressed. She'd slept in later than she meant to, thanks to Clint. But the nap had left her feeling good. She'd be all smiles if not for one thing: she'd sold Coaster. The deal had been finalized yesterday afternoon.

"Let me warm up some pancakes," Gigi said when Sam made it downstairs.

"That's not necessary," Sam said, helping herself to some coffee.

"Nonsense," Gigi said, pulling out a chair. "I just need to warm them up."

Clint's grandmother just about forced her into a chair. Less than five minutes later, pancakes with whip cream smiley faces were set in front of her.

"Gigi, you're too much."

"Just trying to keep a grin on your face." Her expression sobered. "Clint tells me you sold your horse."

Sam nodded. "It was a great offer. I couldn't refuse."

Gigi studied her. "Clint said you seemed upset about it yesterday morning."

"No, no," Sam said quickly, picking up a fork. "Well, maybe I was at first, but it was just the shock of it." She forced a smile. "It's an answer to my prayers, actually, so it's good news."

Another long look. "Okay then. As long as it makes you happy." She tapped the table with her finger. "Eat up."

Sam did as asked, thinking to herself that it was true. She should be thrilled about Coaster finding a new home. With the money from Coaster's sale, she could pay off her medical bills, maybe even have some left over and put the rest away. Her disability coverage wouldn't pay for everything, but if she moved to a less expensive apartment, watched what she spent, she'd be okay. She'd have to move anyway, once her vision gave out. Somewhere closer to a Center for the Blind.

She clenched her hand around the fork.

She *would not* think about it. She would enjoy the day. "Do you know where Clint is?" she asked.

"Getting ready for the big day tomorrow," Gigi said with a wide smile. "He'll be busy getting gear together, choosing what horses will go, probably running to town to get last-minute items."

"Can I help?"

Gigi shook her head. "Don't be silly, dear. You're our guest."

"But you said the other day that I could," Sam said, wagging a finger at her. "Surely there's something I can do."

"You can stay close to the house," Gigi said. "We'll be getting deliveries all day—food supplies, feed for the horses, equipment Clint might have forgotten and that he can con someone into bringing out here. You can let us know when one of those deliveries arrives. I'll be running around today like a chicken with my head cut off."

"Are you going along?" Sam asked, delighted.

"Of course," she said. "I help cook. A family friend brings in a team of draft horses every year. We hook them up to a chuckwagon."

"A chuckwagon?" Sam asked. "You mean with a canvas cover and buckboard sides?"

Gigi wiped her hands down her ever-present apron. "One and the same."

"I'll be darned."

"It's tradition. I used to ride out with the boys, not that my husband liked it. 'Roundup's no place for a woman,' he used to say," her voice low so that she sounded like a grumbling man. "'Kitchen's where women belong.'"

When Gigi saw the look on her face, she quickly
laughed and shook her head. "He was kidding, of
course, but I forced him to put his money where his
mouth was. I demanded to man the kitchen… or the
chuckwagon as the case may be. Next roundup, I ap-
pointed myself cook. And if you've never prepared
meals for a gaggle of hungry men, you've never done
an honest day's work. I sometimes think I should have
stuck to riding."

Sam smiled. "Well, this year you'll have some help."

"I look forward to it," Gigi said. "Anyway, stay close
to the house. Things will be a tad chaotic today."

It was all Gigi would let her do. Sam tried to help out,
even tried to do the dishes when they were done eating,
but Gigi wouldn't hear of it. So she stayed inside, looking
out the front window and hoping Clint might come in for
lunch. He didn't, something she told herself wasn't all
that odd. They were leaving tomorrow. On the roundup.

Tomorrow.

A week from now, she'd be leaving this place, she
thought. And though it seemed impossible to believe,
given that she'd barely just arrived, it would feel as if
she were leaving home…again.

She busied herself for the rest of the day. It was, as
Gigi had said it would be, a crazy day. People were con-
stantly in and out of the house. There was a steady
stream of deliveries all afternoon.

Sam had left the house earlier—just for a little
while—and she'd realized instantly why Gigi had asked
her to stay inside. She'd been in the way, even only
going out to visit the horses. She'd only had time to take
in the camping gear in the barn aisle. A huge wagon sat
outside, though what type of horse was going to pull it,
she had no idea.

"Sam," Gigi called from upstairs. "Gonna need your help. Looks like that horse van has arrived. Clint could probably use an extra pair of hands."

Sam glanced out the window, her attention captured by a big rig coming up the driveway, its white sides glaringly bright. "No problem!" she replied, glad to be doing something at last.

It was warmer outside than it was inside, with a sky as blue as Clint's eyes. But around the edge of that sky was an ever increasing band of darkness...her vision. Failing. It was hard to describe. Where in the middle there was blue, around the edges there was a sort of colorless gray.

Clint was coming out of the barn, instantly recognizable in his beige hat with the eagle feathers sticking out of the side. She felt a smile come to her face, recalling what it'd felt like to have his mouth cover her own...and other places.

"Sam," he said, waving her over.

The sound of the big rig grew ever louder. Sam spied the name of a nationwide equine transportation company on the side. It looked like a rock star van, with darkened windows for the horses inside the trailer. The brakes hissed as the driver came to a stop in front of the barn.

"Looks like quite a load," she said to Clint, wanting to go up to him, to slip into his arms. But it was the first time she'd seen him all day and suddenly she was filled with the most excruciating sense of morning-after-embarrassment.

"Oh, yeah," he said, his eyes sweeping her up and down. And then he raised one of his blond eyebrows, his eyes twinkling as he added, "Gigi tried to get me to check on you again last night."

Sheesh. The man could make her blush. "Why didn't you?" she asked, glancing around. A few of the ranch hands were walking toward them, undoubtedly to help them unload horses.

He leaned toward her and said, "Believe me, I almost did, but I don't want to rush you."

She had to look away for a second. "You're not rushing me."

"Good, 'cause I'm hoping to check on you tonight."

Only then did she admit to herself that she'd been worried he might regret what had happened. Obviously, he didn't.

"Come on," he said. "Here comes Gigi. I think she wants you to unload the new horse."

She frowned. "Horse? I thought they were the draft horses for the chuckwagon or something."

Clint shook his head. "Not this load," he said. "This is a horse Gigi bought. Told me about it this morning. I think you'll like him."

The driver of the van was walking toward them. "What kind of horse is it?" she asked.

"You'll see."

"You Clint McAlister?" the driver asked, a heavyset man who looked as though he spent a lot of time behind the wheel.

"I am."

"Got your new horse here."

Clint took the clipboard the man offered, and the pen, signing his name with a flourish. Another guy was pulling a ramp out from the middle of the trailer. By now, Sam was dying of curiosity.

"Is it a horse for Gigi to ride?" she asked.

"Nope. It's some fancy show horse," Clint said. "Gigi saw an ad on the Internet and fell in love. Bought the horse yesterday morning, although *she* just told about it last night…*after* you went to bed."

And Sam knew. She turned toward the van. The door above the ramp opened.

"No," she said softly. They couldn't have.

But once the door opened, she was able to see the front end of the animal inside…a familiar black head, ears pricked forward, nostrils flaring.

"Oh, God."

"Happy birthday, Sam," Clint said gently.

"No," she said, clasping her cheeks. "No, no, no… you didn't."

"Didn't what?" Gigi asked. "Buy myself a show horse? I sure did. Heard he was a real nice one, too."

She couldn't see, but not because her eyes had given out, but because tears clouded her vision. The man inside the trailer opened a door holding Coaster in a tiny stall, unclipped him from his cross-ties, and in the next instant Sam knew they had, indeed, brought her horse to her.

"Wire transfer went through this morning," Gigi said, a huge smile on her face. "But you're to consider the money we paid for him a loan. You can pay us back a little at a time, or not at all, up to you. But he's still yours. If you want him."

"If I want him." She didn't know what to say, what to do. Did she run forward and take the lead of her horse, wrap her arms around Coaster and tell him how much she missed him? Or did she turn to the people who'd given him back to her. The heavenly, wonderful people who she'd met just days ago, but had taken her into their hearts.

"I don't know how to thank you," she told Gigi because if she looked at Clint, she'd break down. "I just have no clue what to say." To hell with it. She let the tears come, falling into Gigi's arms without conscious thought.

"We thought you could use a break," Gigi said, her own voice sounding suspiciously thick. "You've had such a hard time of it."

Sam drew back. "But *twenty thousand dollars!*"

"Shh," Gigi said. "We can afford it. Or should I say, Clint can afford it."

Sam glanced at Clint…and the man who'd brought her to such amazing heights, but who'd made her heart sing in an altogether different way this afternoon. "Clint?" she said. "Did you buy him for me?"

"Well," Clint said, lifting his hat and running a hand through his hair. "It was Gigi's idea, but it was the ranch that bought him and so I had to sign the check—so to speak. We did a wire transfer this morning."

"You mean you knew about this the whole time?"

"No," he said quickly. "Gigi admitted what she'd done after I told her how upset you were. She begged me not to tell you last night."

"I hope you don't mind," Gigi said. "I wanted to surprise you."

Mind? How could she mind?

"It took a lot of work on your broker's part to get Coaster here by this afternoon," Clint said. "And I don't know if you should be happy or horrified that he took us at our word that we were good for the money…poor horse was on a van all night."

"You might want to turn him loose in the arena," Gigi said. "Let him stretch out a bit."

Sam stared between two of the most amazing people she'd ever met. "How can I ever repay you?" she asked, wiping at her cheeks. "I mean, how can I ever—"

"Shh," Gigi said a second time. "We know you'll do your best to pay us back. But if you decide it's too much work to pay us back, we'll make other arrangements. We just didn't want you to have to lose your horse. Not after everything you've already been through."

She felt tears burn her eyes again. "You two…"

"Like I said," Clint told her, "It was Gigi's idea."

Sam went to Gigi and gave her a hug.

"But it was Clint's money," Gigi said when she stepped back.

Sam faced the man she barely knew, yet who already held a special place in her heart. "Thank you," she said, moving into his arms.

He hugged her tight, as he said softly, "Don't thank me just yet. You haven't heard how I expect you to pay me back."

Sam leaned away from him. "Oh, I have a fair idea what you'll want me to do…and I'll be only too happy to provide."

"Will you now?"

"Tonight."

"I'm looking forward to it."

Chapter Fourteen

Clint wasn't going to force himself on Sam—and that's what it would feel like he was doing if he let her make good on her promise. Besides, he thought as he watched her throw her arms around her horse, and bury her nose in his neck. They had all the time in the world.

It was a jubilant Gigi who watched Sam take Coaster's lead. The whole damn ranch had come to a standstill.

"That's a big horse," Elliot said. The stooped old cowboy stroked her chin as if contemplating just how difficult it might be to mount such an animal.

"Shee-uut," Dean said. "That ain't a horse. That's a giraffe."

Clint had to agree. It was hard to believe that the short and stocky quarter horse could come in such a large package.

Sam clucked, steering the horse toward him, her smile as big as the sky above them. "This," she said with a wave of her hand toward the crowd at large, "is Coaster."

"He's beautiful, Sam," Gigi said.

"I'm glad you think so…since he's yours."

"Now, now," his grandmother said. "Enough of that. The horse is yours, no matter what the bill of sale says."

But Sam was shaking her head. "A deal's a deal. He's yours, at least until I can pay you back, which I promise to do." Her smile faded a little and Clint knew she was thinking…*somehow.*

"Yeah, well, one of these days you'll have to show us what he can do," he said.

"How about you ride him since you own him," she suggested.

"No, thanks. I like my western saddles."

"You could ride him western," she insisted. "He's a quarter horse, remember?"

When Gigi laughed, Clint glanced over at her. His grandmother looked tickled to pieces—and it was such a pleasure to see. She hadn't laughed like that since, well, since his grandfather had died.

"She has a point, Clint," Gigi said. "I say you should ride him."

"No." Clint shook his head.

"Chicken?" Sam taunted.

"Smart," Clint contradicted.

"Fine. I'll ride him in a western saddle. I'll even take him out on a trail to prove to you that the fancy show horse you own is, in fact, a horse bred to chase cows, no matter what his size."

"That horse chasing cows is something I'd like to see," Dean called out.

"Deal."

"But, Sam," Gigi said, switching suddenly into mother-mode. "You have no idea how that horse of yours will react."

"It's *your* horse," she repeated. "And I suspect he'll react just fine. He's seen cows at the shows. So as long as you don't mind me trying something new with *your* horse, I'm game to try."

"I'm sure you are," Gigi said. "But let's take it slow, okay? Sure, a trail ride today, that'll be good for him. He can stretch his legs after his long journey."

"Actually, I was thinking of taking Coaster on the roundup…if that's okay with you."

"No," Clint said. "You have no idea how your horse is going to react out on a trail. Creeks, wildlife and rough terrain—no place for a fancy animal like that."

"He's a horse," she said, "not a show dog. He'll do just fine."

"No."

"Gigi," she implored, turning toward his grandmother.

"I have to agree with Clint on this one," the woman said.

Sam's gaze darted between the two of them. "How about if I prove it to you."

"Prove it *how?*" Clint asked.

"Like Gigi suggested, when you're done with work today, meet me at the arena. We'll move some cattle inside there."

"We haven't brought any cattle down from pasture."

"I'll bring a few head in," Dean offered.

"Dean." Clint shook his head.

"What?" the young ranch hand asked. "I wanna watch a rodeo tonight."

Clint crossed his arms. "Don't you have work to do?"

Dean looked at him sheepishly. "I was just offering to help."

"We don't need your help."

"Actually," Sam said, "if he wants to move some cows for me, that'd be great." Her horse tossed its head impatiently. Sam soothed him with a kind hand. "See. He wants to go play, too. Don't you, boy?"

"We'll talk about it later," Clint said. "Right now, we all need to get back to work." He looked at the employees that'd gathered around. "Go on," he said. "We're heading out tomorrow at dawn. Let's make sure we're ready."

"Speaking of that," Gigi said, "I still have my own packing to do."

Which left him alone with Sam. "You're not going to take that horse of yours out on the trail."

"Oh yeah?" she asked, fishing the lead line through her hand so she could scoot closer. "You going to ground me in the house to keep me off him."

He was half-tempted to pull her into his arms to kiss the sassiness off her face.

"Yeah, to your room," he said softly, but the words were a mistake because the minute he said them, he was reminded of what had happened yesterday morning— in her *room*—and how much he wanted to do the same thing tonight.

"Is that a threat? Or a promise?"

"Take it as you will," he said. But he couldn't stop himself from touching her. "Go ride your horse," he said. "Get some practice time in. But *no* cows."

"Will you join me?"

"Wish I could," he said. "I've got too much work to do. But I'll see you tonight."

"After dinner?" she asked suggestively.

"Maybe."

"Maybe?" Her eyebrows arched.

"It's going to be a long day, Sam. Honestly, I don't know if I'm going to have the energy to do much more than crawl between the covers."

"I see," she said. "You're the love-'em-and-leave-'em type."

"No," he said on a huff of laughter. "I'm the let's-take-things-slow type."

"And what if I'm the take-things-fast type?" She smiled up at him flirtatiously.

"I would say slow down, champ. We have all the time in the world."

Something changed in her face, something he might not have noticed if he hadn't been watching her carefully.

"What is it?" he asked. "What'd I say?"

"Nothing," she said quickly. "Nothing at all. I was just thinking you're right. You've got a lot to do. We'll be leaving tomorrow. I should be letting you get back to work."

"Hey, wait," he said when she turned away, Coaster following meekly behind. "Sam," he called out again.

Reluctantly she faced him.

"Don't look at me like that," he said gently. "I'll see you later. And, who knows, I might just have enough energy to kiss you senseless again."

She smiled wanly. "Don't mind me," she said, running back and kissing him on the cheek. "I think I'm just overwhelmed by everything that's happening."

"Well, I can certainly understand that," he said, rubbing her upper arm. His ranch hands were watching and he knew he was going to be teased about that peck she'd just given him.

Jealous. They'd all be jealous.

"Go on," he said. "Ride your horse. *Away from the cows.* I'll peek in on you in a bit."

WE HAVE ALL THE TIME in the world.

But what if they didn't? Sam thought, leading Coaster to the barn so she could tack him up. What if, like so many other things in her life, something changed…

something radical and unexpected—like her vision. God, she hadn't even told him about her eyes.

Hey, Clint, thanks for jumping into bed with me. Did I mention I'm going blind?

She paused at the entrance to the barn, ostensibly to let Coaster sniff the interior, but there was another reason. It'd gotten to be a habit of hers. She would pause for a moment and let her eyes adjust to the sudden darkness, allowing herself to feel—just for an instant—what it was going to be like when the world went dark. *Permanently,* went dark.

"Maybe *he* has all the time in the world," she said, looking over at Coaster. "But I don't."

She knew what she was about to do would make him mad. It might even make him mad enough to leave her home tomorrow. But she honestly couldn't think of another way to convince Clint that Coaster could be trusted on the trail. And doing exactly that suddenly became critical to her. Once her vision went away, she wouldn't be riding again, not unless someone led her around. This might be one of her last chances to do something with Coaster that she could remember forever—in her mind's eye.

So she tacked up her horse. When she was finished, she looked up and down that barn aisle and nonchalantly closed off one end of the barn.

Someone did look up. She just smiled sheepishly and said, "Too drafty," and the guy went right back to work.

To be honest, people were coming and going from all over. Dean and Elliot and a bunch of the other ranch hands were setting out gear or fitting saddles to the horses. There were packs on the ground, grain bags for the horses, sleeping bags, canvas covers and what looked to be tents. Clint was gone, she'd been told. Off to pull in some horses from the pasture to use on their ride.

Her timing couldn't be more perfect.

She slipped between the massive double doors. She knew how to work cattle chutes. Her trainer back in Delaware specialized in all types of show events, even ones that involved cattle, and so she'd lent a hand or two there. It was a simple matter to push a few of the yearling Herefords into an alleyway, then close them off. Even more simple to open the chutes ahead of those cows, then force them through. In a matter of minutes, she had five mooing, mad, brown-and-white steers in the arena.

"Shh," she ordered, glancing back at the barn.

The doors were still closed and no one had noticed what she was doing. Her biggest fear was Clint returning, or Gigi spying her from the house.

"Okay, Coaster," she told her horse once she snuck back into the barn, "I know we're in a western saddle, but you can do this. We'll show Clint and Gigi."

Her horse seemed to eye her as if he knew she was up to no good. She almost laughed. Truly, she shared a bond with Coaster unlike any other. Her horse could do anything.

This would be fun. And maybe, if she was lucky, Clint would catch her doing it. She could prove to him that Coaster had what it took to be a ranch horse.

"Come on," she said, opening one side of the barn doors and slipping out.

The cows were right where she left them. Coaster gave them hardly a look.

"See," she told no one in particular, "this is going to be a piece of cake."

Slipping into the arena proved to be the tricky part. Once the cows caught sight of her, they started running around. She had a second or two where she thought they'd come right at her, but they kept to one end.

"All-righty," she said, studying Coaster. Funny, she'd never thought of her horse as being particularly big, but with that big old western saddle on him, he was closer to eighteen hands than seventeen. "Looks like we'll need to use the fence."

She glanced toward the house, convinced Gigi would come running toward her any minute now. When that didn't happen, she glanced toward the rolling hills. No sign of Clint.

Coaster was busy staring at the cows and so he stood still as she climbed the fence, and then into the saddle. He wasn't afraid of them, just curious. She clucked him forward.

"What the *hell* do you think you're doing?"

Son of a—

She swiveled in the saddle. "Hey, Clint," she said, smiling.

"Samantha, get down off that horse."

"Why?" she asked. "You can see Coaster's going to be fine. He's not even looking at them."

Well, that wasn't exactly true. Her horse was very definitely staring, but it was no big deal.

"Sam," Clint said in a non-nonsense, dead calm voice. "Get down from that horse now."

There was one thing about Sam that Clint didn't know. She had a stubborn streak a mile wide. "I'm just going to push the cows around for a little while," she said. "Prove to you that old Coaster here can be a ranch horse."

"Sam," he repeated.

But Sam cued Coaster for a trot, and, being the obedient show horse that he was, Coaster went straight for the brown-and-white cows, head down, which was the quarter horse way to go. She knew immediately that he wasn't as committed to the idea of working with steers as she was. "C'mon, boy. We can do this."

But her horse had had enough. He stopped at least twenty feet away, head lowered, a loud snort coming from his nostrils.

"See," Clint called. "Bad idea. Come out this instant."

Sam just patted Coaster's neck. She was in a western saddle. The thing had a horn. If she got in trouble, she'd just hold on. "It's okay, Coaster. It's just cows. No big deal."

Her heart was pumping. To be honest, she hadn't felt this alive since…well…since before the accident. There'd be hell to pay, but she was a terrific rider—if only Clint would give her a chance to prove herself.

Her horse took a step forward, his head still low, his breath still coming out in snorts, but Coaster trusted her. One of the steers at the end of the arena broke free. Sam tensed, having anticipated the move. Would Coaster run? Or would he hold his ground?

He held his ground.

"Good boy," she called as the steer in question made a strafing run for the other end. Its buddies called out.

Now came the real test, sending Coaster after the cow. She would need to chase it back to the herd. Pulling on the reins, she pointed the gelding toward the far end of the arena. He meekly trotted in that direction. A lone cow didn't seem to concern him as much as a whole herd.

"Good boy," she told him.

Something must have clicked. Some long-forgotten genetic memory that switched on in Coaster's mind because suddenly her English riding horse was eyeing that cow like it was a gunslinger at the O.K. Corral. The cow ducked right. Coaster followed.

"Hah," she cried, glancing in Clint's direction. "I told you he could do this."

She followed after the steer, returning it to the herd. Another one broke free. She sent Coaster after it. Her horse still wasn't too sure about that group of steers at the end of the arena, but he had no problem chasing after the lone deserter. This time Coaster *ran*. Sam found herself at the opposite end of the arena in no time. The cow rounded one corner, toward the left. So did Coaster. But then the cow turned back, abruptly facing Coaster.

"Crap!" she cried.

But her horse didn't freak. He pinned his ears, and as the cow slid past, he spun on his backend. It was a move that would have done a cutting horse proud, but Sam wasn't ready for it.

She was off balance, and as Coaster set off after the cow, she became even *more* off balance.

"Sam!" she heard Clint yell.

She was going to fall. Damn it. But having come off a horse more than a few times before, she knew what needed to be done. Curling her body into itself, she dove for the ground.

She hit with an oomph that would have done a cartoon character proud.

Clint was right beside her. "You fool, idiot, *stubborn* woman."

But she was laughing. "Did you see that?" she asked, moving first one leg and then the other. All seemed to be in working order. She sat up on her elbows.

"Don't move," Clint said.

"I'm fine." She pushed herself to her feet.

Coaster was only a few paces away, looking at her as if he was shocked she'd fallen off him. "That was incredible. He actually chased that cow."

"You could have broken your neck."

"Boxing cows?" she asked, moving to catch Coaster's reins. "Don't be silly."

He stepped in front of her, his eyes all but spitting fire. "What were you thinking?"

"Coaster can make a ranch horse."

"By chasing cattle?" he asked. "Lady, it takes a lot more than that to prove a horse's mettle."

"What other untrained animal would go after a steer like that?"

"I don't care if he looks good enough to win the National Cutting Horse Futurity. It was a damn, stupid thing to do."

"Clint, I'm fine," she said, reaching out to touch his arm.

"Because you were lucky."

"Riding horses is risky," she said. "Always. The truth is I have less chance of getting hurt here, in a soft, sand arena, than I do out there."

"You're right," he shot back. "It's going to be too dangerous for you out there. You can't go."

"What!" she cried. "You can't do that."

"Yes, I can." He crammed his hat down on his head. "I own this ranch and I can do whatever I want."

"No, you don't. Gigi owns this place."

He leaned toward her. "Wrong." He glanced at Coaster. "Bring that horse back to the barn. You're through working cows for the day."

"But, I—"

"Bring him back or you'll never get on him again."

"You wouldn't do that," she said, tipping her chin up. Yes, she knew she'd been reckless. All right, maybe even irresponsible, too, but he didn't need to come down on her so hard.

I own this ranch.

How had she managed to miss that? Why hadn't Gigi told her? Why hadn't Clint?

"Yes, I would," he said, a vein on the side of his neck popping out. "I own him, remember?" He turned away.

"Clint—"

He ignored her. Sam was left standing in the arena with nothing but Coaster and a few cows to keep her company. "Darn."

Chapter Fifteen

"You're being too hard on her," Gigi told him later.

"Too hard on her?" Clint said, stuffing work shirts into the canvas duffel he'd be strapping to his saddle tomorrow. "We hadn't even left the ranch yet and she's already disobeying me."

"She was trying to prove a point."

Clint faced her. Eyes nearly as blue as his own stared back at him. "Don't tell me you're taking her side?"

"I just understand her reasons for doing what she did. Sometimes you've got to take the bull by the horns, especially with the men in this family."

"She shouldn't have done it," Clint said, returning to his task.

"No, she shouldn't have. You're right. But she's an excellent rider and she didn't get hurt. And for some reason, it's important she ride that horse of hers on the roundup."

"I didn't buy that horse from her so she could put herself in danger."

"Actually, *I* arranged to buy the horse. But you were the one who called that horse broker at least twenty times to make sure he'd get here in time for the roundup. If you didn't want her to ride him, why'd you push so hard?"

He shrugged, refusing to answer the question. But Gigi was like a dog with a bone.

"Why, Clint, if you weren't thinking she might be able to use him this week?"

He shook his head. "If I thought that—" he glanced over his shoulder "—if, I changed my mind the minute I clapped eyes on him. He's too big for trail riding."

"Bullpucky."

He whipped around to face her. "Yes, he is. Too showy, too."

"Too showy?" Gigi asked, exasperated. "Now you sound like a damn fool."

He shook his head. "It's too dangerous out there for her."

"You're starting to care for her."

"Of course I care for her. I wouldn't have paid a fortune for her horse if I didn't care for her. I'd have to have veins full of ice not to feel sorry for the woman."

"You don't feel sorry for her," Gigi said, "and you know it." She held up her hands. "I know, I know, there's a part of you that sympathizes with what she's going through, but Clinton, I've never known you to be intimate with a woman without having feelings for her first."

"I *haven't* been intimate with her."

"No?" she asked, and it was the same look she'd given him when he'd stashed a snake in his room…and then denied it to her face.

"No," he said, moving to his dresser. "Not really. Oh, I don't know what the hell to say to you except leave me alone already. I need to pack."

"You only just met her, but she's already slipped under your defenses. I can tell. What's more, watching her fall off that horse of hers today about scared you to death."

"I've seen people come off horses before," he muttered.

"Yes, but not someone you care for. Julia flat out refused to ride and that's the closest you've ever come to settling down. Thank God you came to your senses beforehand."

"We're not talking about Julia."

"And you're acting like a recalcitrant child," Gigi said, coming into his room and forcing him to turn and look at her. "Let her ride her horse tomorrow. She'll be fine."

"Knock, knock."

They both glanced at the door. Sam.

"I'll just leave the two of you alone," Gigi said. But his grandmother shot him a look that clearly said, *be nice to her.*

Yeah, yeah, yeah.

Gigi left behind what felt like twenty tons of silence. Clint went back to packing.

"I'm sorry," she said softly.

"It's fine."

But you're still not going on the roundup.

He wanted to say the words out loud, he truly did, but he realized Gigi was right. He *did* care for her. Damn. How the hell had that happened so fast?

"No, it's not fine. You told me not to do it, and I did."

"We all make mistakes," he said, wanting to stay angry with her, but he couldn't do it. She appeared beyond miserable, and it was exactly that look—that expression of misery—that'd gotten him into trouble in the first place. He just couldn't seem to stop himself from wanting to erase her sadness.

"It was reckless of me to do what I did. On a horse I don't even own…not anymore. But there was a reason why I did it."

"I'm sure there was," he said, trying—and failing—to maintain his stern facade.

But she wasn't looking at him, not now. She was staring out the window behind him. His room was much like hers. Bed to the right, window next to that, dresser on the wall opposite the bed. As she gazed out that window, he saw the most gut-wrenching look of loss cross her face.

"What is it?" he asked, instantly alert. She wasn't about to tell him she was engaged or something, was she? He hadn't started to care for yet another woman who didn't know the meaning of fidelity, had he?

"I'm going blind."

He gaped at her.

They were not the words he was expecting and he found himself saying, "What?" just so he could make sure he'd heard her correctly. "You're going where?"

"Blind," she said. "I'm going blind."

"But you're—" He was about to say "fine." That she appeared to be okay.

I'm still recovering from my injuries.

"It's true," she said. "After I woke up, I kept telling the doctors something wasn't right with my eyes. My peripheral vision wasn't there. It took yet another brain scan to narrow it down to a central retinal vein occlusion brought on by a brain embolism. They're almost positive the embolism was the result of the car accident. I was bleeding inside my head and they theorize a blood clot migrated to my retinal artery, but of course no one can say with any certainty. They also can't tell me why it's getting bigger, only that it's there."

"Can't they do something about it?" he asked because he just couldn't believe she was going blind.

She shook her head. "They tried blasting it apart with some kind of new-fangled ultrasonic device, but it didn't work. Short of drilling a hole in my head, no. They already did that once," she said, running a hand through her short curls. "It used to be past my shoulders."

He stared at her in disbelief.

"So when you said you knew I'd been going through a rough patch, you had no idea just how rough that patch has been."

"You're going blind," he said, still not wanting to believe it.

"Slowly, but inexorably," she said. "Taking Coaster out today, it might be my last time to try my hand at something new. Tomorrow might be the day my vision gets to the critical point."

"Good grief." He knew it wasn't the best thing to say under the circumstances. Knew he should pull her into his arms, but that seemed so inadequate.

"And that's why I'd really like to take Coaster out on the roundup if I'm able," she said. "You guys have no idea what a gift it was for you to bring him here. I never thought I'd see him again, but now I might be able to take him out. To see the hills…and the horses. I want to go on one last adventure with him. One last gallop across the fields."

He went to her then, couldn't help but do anything else. "You sound incredibly brave."

She shrugged. "I don't feel brave."

Clint met her gaze and thought how impossible it seemed that those stunning green eyes would one day be sightless. Would he be able to read what she was thinking then? Would they seem to sparkle like they did now? Or would they go dim? Like a window suddenly closed.

"You're the bravest person I know," he said, hugging her. God, when he'd seen her in that arena, about to chase those cows, he'd been horrified. And impressed.

"Can I go on the roundup?" she asked.

"You know you can," he said, pulling her closer.

But she wiggled away from him. "Don't," she said. "Not now. If you hold me now, I might crumple and I've sworn never to do that again."

He stood there, helpless. "Is there anything I can do?"

"Yeah. Don't treat me like I'm made from glass."

His gut kicked. "I won't."

She turned to go.

"Sam—"

But he could tell she didn't trust herself not to lose control if he said something kind.

"Damn," he muttered after she'd disappeared out the door. Now what to do?

"SHE'S WHAT?" GIGI SAID when he tracked her down in the basement less than fifteen minutes later. "Going blind?"

Clint nodded, took his hat off his head and scrubbed a hand over his face. "Said she didn't know when it was going to happen, that it was supposed to happen gradually. But I imagine that was a big reason why she sold her horse."

"My goodness," Gigi said. There was a window to the right of the walk-in pantry, a tiny rectangular one, but it allowed enough light into the basement to reveal Gigi's stricken expression.

"Honestly, Gigi, I didn't know what to do. What to say."

His grandmother shook her head, nibbling her lower lip. "Neither do I," she said, looking around for something. The basement was more of a storeroom. He saw her spot whatever it was she was looking for. A chair, he realized. Gigi sank into it.

"What can we do for her?" she asked, her blue eyes wide.

"I asked her the same question. She said not to treat her like she was made of glass."

Gigi nodded slowly.

"I'll have to admit, Gigi, I'm not too sure she should go on that roundup now."

"What?" Gigi asked. "Don't be ridiculous. That roundup is probably all she has to look forward to. Don't you see?" she said. "It's why she came here. She wanted to see the mustangs before she—" Gigi covered her mouth with her hand again. "Goes blind," she said from between her fingers. "Heavens to Betsy. That sounds so horrible."

He hadn't thought about that yet, Clint admitted. Hadn't had a chance to do much more than assimilate what Sam had told him. "So you think she should go?"

"Of course I do. We'll have to keep a close eye on her, but she has to go…now more than ever."

But Clint still didn't like it. Honestly, he felt as if he'd been poleaxed. What kind of woman showed up at a ranch and foisted herself on strangers knowing the whole time she was going blind?

A frightened woman, he realized. One who'd had nowhere else to turn, and no place to run.

Chapter Sixteen

She'd told him.

She'd *had* to tell him.

But as she lay in bed that night, she regretted it. Not because she was afraid her blindness might turn Clint off, or that he might be afraid to get close to her....

All right, fine.

That was a very *real* concern, especially since he seemed to avoid her for the rest of the day. He didn't even knock on her door the whole long night.

Gigi had told her to report to the barn at six with her bag in hand. The house was quiet as a library when Sam grabbed her jacket from the coatrack near the front door and the black duffel bag Gigi had let her borrow.

It was cool outside, but she felt well protected from the elements. She wore her most comfortable boots and as many layers of clothing as she could tolerate, but being late April, the sky was still dark, the horizon nothing more than a dull, gunmetal-gray. Overhead, stars still twinkled. And as she had so many times in the previous months, she took a mental picture of everything.

A rooster crowed in the distance. Sam took a deep breath. Long after she left here, she would remember that smell of the place. A combination of fresh-cut hay, pine-scented horse shavings and the pungent daisies next to the house.

"You ready?" Dean asked as she entered the barn. The fluorescent light that stretched up the barn aisle buzzed as if it'd just been turned on.

"As ready as I'll ever be."

Dean smiled. "Heard you fell off yesterday."

"My fault. My horse was boxing a cow and I wasn't ready for him."

"Clint said he's never seen someone come off so gracefully."

Graceful? That's what he'd called it? She sure wouldn't have guessed that after looking into his eyes. "Yeah, well, I like to jump horses. Can't tell you how many times the horse decided it didn't want to go over a fence at the last moment. Usually I kept going right on over that horse's head."

Dean winced. "Speaking of your horse, Clint said for you to go ahead and saddle Coaster."

So she would get to ride him after all. Sam nodded, feeling the knot in her stomach unwind.

"Where's Clint?" she asked, glancing around. She would bet Gigi was out by the chuckwagon making sure she had all her supplies, but he was nowhere to be seen.

"In the arena. That's where we stage all the horses before we go."

Ah. "Well okay then. I better saddle up."

Sam was nervous. Whether or not they'd catch up with the Baer Mountain Mustangs today, she had no idea. But sooner or later, she'd get to see them. In the meantime she was going to cross some rough terrain, on an unproven horse. Not that she had any fears about Coaster. Okay, maybe just a few, but worse case, she could turn back. Or maybe Clint had thought to bring an extra horse. She'd have to ask him about that.

By the time she finished saddling Coaster, men were leading horses out of the arena. She could see them through the barn's double doors. The sun had climbed higher in the horizon, turning everything a sort of muted gold. She paused and admired the view. It looked like a scene from an Old West movie. Long-coated cowboys, all of them wearing western hats, milling around on horseback. In the center of the action Clint sat his dapple gray. The gelding was easy to spot among so many bays and chestnuts. Behind him on the chuckwagon, Gigi's white hair was clearly visible. She wasn't driving. That job fell to a grizzled cowboy who made Elliot appear a stripling.

"You ready?" someone asked her. She shook her head slowly as she took it all in.

"I'm ready," she said.

"You need a boost up?" the man asked.

She had no idea who the guy was. "No. That's okay." Whoever he was, he was about Clint's age, and handsome, if one was into movie star good looks. Really. He was too pretty to be a cowboy with his brown eyes and cleft chin. "I don't see a crane around here," he joked, eyeing Coaster behind her.

"Believe me," she said, "I'm used to getting on him."

"Well, have at it. Looks like Clint is ready to head out."

And he hadn't even said good morning to her yet. Of course, he was busy, but she couldn't help but wonder if things had changed between them. That other morning in her bedroom seemed like nothing more than a distant memory, and while she hadn't expected him to come into her room and give her a good-night kiss last night, she'd been hoping to see him before she went to bed. All she'd seen was Gigi.

"All right, Coaster," Sam said, putting her left foot in the stirrup. "No sudden turns today."

If her horse thought it was strange to be wearing a different type of saddle again, he never gave anything away. Honestly, the western seat was far more comfortable than its tiny English counterpart. She felt as if she was sitting in a lounge chair.

"...remember, last one through the gate has to make sure it's closed. I don't need to tell you what a mess we'd have on our hands if the horses escaped to the wrong pasture, so be on the ball."

Clint's eyes fell on her. She smiled. He nodded, then said to his men, "If we're all ready, let's head on out. Cappie, you go first."

"Cappie" appeared to be the chuckwagon driver because he lifted his hand and then flicked a whip over his horse's back.

And that was that. They were off. Sam kept expecting Clint to hang back. He didn't. She told herself not to feel hurt. He was busy. The last thing he was going to do was blow kisses at her. It was just silly to expect that, and yet for some ridiculous reason, she kind of did. She would have been happy with just a smile.

The man who'd teased her about getting up on Coaster sidled next to her, his brown eyes twinkling. She glanced down at him—and it *was* down—the horse he was riding was closer to a pony.

"I'm Lorenzo," he said, holding out a hand, his leg bumping the rope tied to the front of his saddle. They all had ropes—except her—not that she'd know how to use it.

She had to lean down and twist her body to take it. "Hi," she said. "I'm Sam."

He smiled, his grin teeth-whitening commercial bright.

Wow. With his dark skin and dark eyes, he looked as if he belonged on the set of a spaghetti Western, especially in his cowboy attire.

"Is that your horse?" he asked.

How to answer *that?* Obviously, he hadn't heard the story. That meant he wasn't one of Clint's regulars, but a day worker, something Gigi had explained was a cowboy for hire. "No," she said. "He belongs to the ranch."

"Really. He looks like a show horse."

That piqued her curiosity about him. "Actually, he *is* a show horse. He's been shown on the quarter horse circuit…."

She gave him Coaster's background as they rode along. And if Lorenzo—she couldn't believe his name was *Lorenzo,* as though he was some kind of Italian soap star or something—thought it odd that she knew so much about a horse that wasn't hers, he didn't say anything. And, frankly, it was nice to talk to someone during the long trip up the hill. Gigi was hip-deep in conversation with Cappie and she didn't want to intrude. Clint ignored her.

Fortunately, she was distracted by the scenery. They rode toward the Baer Mountains—the green, snow-capped peaks looked like scoops of mint ice cream. The valley they were in curved upward, toward the hills, the incline gradual, but enough of an angle that she was grateful Coaster had been kept in shape during the months she couldn't ride. She, however, had some catching up to do. It took hours to reach the top. She suspected she might be sore tomorrow.

"Best take some aspirin," Lorenzo said when they finally stopped. Obviously, he'd seen her grimace as she'd slid to the ground.

"Thanks. I think I will."

Coaster's halter hung from a strap on the side of her

saddle. She took his bridle off and slipped it on, tying him to a tree. "Keep up the good work," she told the horse, scratching his neck for a couple of seconds. "We'll make a cow pony out of you yet."

"You sure about that?"

She spun on her heel to find Clint staring down at her. "Hey," she said. She'd thought for sure she'd receive the silent treatment until later that night—if not for the rest of the week.

"You look tired. You okay?"

"I'm fine," she said, lifting her chin. *No need to worry about me. Go back to directing the troops.*

But she identified the thought as childish as soon as she thought it.

"If you're hungry," he said, "Cappie'll have the hamburgers grilling in just a sec. Why don't you wait a second and I'll introduce the two of you."

"That's okay," she said. "I can introduce myself."

"Just the same, I'll guide you over to the cart."

She stepped back from him. "Clint, I'm not blind... yet."

He winced.

"You don't need to worry about me," she said, verbalizing the exact thought she'd had earlier. "I'll tell you if my vision starts to change."

"Is that what will happen? It'll just start fading away."

She nodded. "For the most part, yes. I've already lost thirty percent of my peripheral vision. Not enough to lose my driver's license, but enough that I can't see things out of the corner of my eyes. Believe me, if that gets worse, I'll tell you straight away."

He continued to stare down at her, his arms crossed. They stood on a small hill, one that overlooked the valley where his family's ranch sat—correction—*his* ranch sat.

"And when that *does* happen, Sam," he said, "what then? Do we drive you to the airport? Put you on a plane? Slap you on the rear and wish you luck?"

"It won't happen that quickly," she said. "This is a slow progression. Three months ago it was just a bothersome blind spot. Now it's worse. At this rate I have two, maybe three more months before it gets really bad. I expect that by next year I'll be blind." But it could happen sooner…much sooner. They honestly couldn't determine when it would happen, or how quickly. Things could change, they'd said. But she was banking on the fact that it wouldn't happen fast. Of course, she didn't tell Clint that.

"And afterward," he asked. "After you've gone…"

Blind. Come on, Clint. Say the word. You can do it.

"After it happens, what do you plan to do?"

If she'd needed further proof that he was bothered, maybe even repulsed by what was going to happen to her, she had it.

"I'll go to the Delaware Center for the Blind. They'll teach me how to get around, maybe even learn a new vocation. I'll be okay."

"And what if you're not?"

"What do you mean?" she asked, pushing a lock of short hair out of her eyes. It'd gotten breezy all of a sudden.

"What if you have trouble…" He appeared to be searching for a word. "Adjusting."

"You mean what if I become suicidal?"

He blanched. "That's not what I meant. But what happens if you can't cope?"

She'd been asking herself that question ever since she'd been given her diagnosis. "I don't know," she said softly. "I honestly don't know." She recognized in that moment that she was coming to grips with her future.

Spending time with Clint and Gigi had given her unexpected strength. "I guess I'll cross that bridge when I come to it."

She waited for him to say something, maybe something like, "I'll be there…don't you worry."

He had followed her gaze, his face in profile as he stared out at the ranch in front of them. He wore his cowboy hat, of course. The smell of earth and horse clung to him as if he were part of the Montana countryside—and it stirred her desire even after he'd ignored her for half the day.

"I should check the horses' girths," he said.

"Yeah, maybe you should do that," Sam said sharper than she intended.

"Be sure and eat."

He walked away, and with each step he took, he trod on Sam's heart.

Chapter Seventeen

He knew he was being an ass, knew it and yet couldn't seem to stop himself.

"Damn it," he muttered, without paying attention to where he was going.

"Watch out!" someone cried.

Clint stopped just shy of knocking Gigi to the ground. His grandmother steadied herself against the side of the wagon, the twenty-pound sack of potatoes she carried nearly slipping from her gasp.

"Geez, Clint."

"Sorry," he said, quickly taking the sack from her. "Didn't see you."

"Well," she said, hands on her hips. "I'm not surprised judging by the look on that girl's face while you were talking to her."

"What? What look?"

"Did you tell her to gouge her eyes out with something? To go ahead and get it over with maybe?"

"Gigi! What a thing to accuse me of."

"So then. What did you say to her?"

"Nothing. I mean, we just talked."

"Yeah...for the first time all morning."

"I've been busy," he said. But he made the mistake

of glancing back. She still stood where he'd left her, still staring out over the valley.

The sickness returned, that same stomach ache he'd felt when she'd told him what was in store for her. He couldn't imagine… Couldn't even begin to understand… Didn't think he would ever want to know what it would be like to lose his sight.

"Well, whatever you said to her, it's hard to decide who looks worse—you or her."

He shook his head, shifted the potatoes to his other side. "She's got a lot on her mind."

"So do you, if I don't miss my guess."

"Where to?" he asked, ignoring what was very obviously a prompt.

"Just set them over there, near where Cappie is cooking."

He nodded. Gigi always peeled potatoes the day before she and Cappie had to cook them up for breakfast. That way they weren't peeling and chopping by firelight in the early morning.

"You want me to get you a bag of onions, too?" he asked, after setting his load down. Cappie nodded before going back to the hamburger patties on his flat-iron skillet. Cappie kept to himself. Easily eighty years old with gray hair and dark, nearly black eyes, he made his living cooking for ranches on roundups. The man might not be much for conversation, but he sure could cook. Clint's stomach growled when he caught a whiff of onion and garlic.

"You looking for something else to do?" Gigi asked.

"Actually, I was going to check the horses' girths."

He needed to keep busy. Needed to find a way to stop thinking about *her.* Now that they were underway, there wasn't much for him to do other than keep an eye on things. Most of the guys had been on the trail with them before and so they knew each other. Only Sam and Lorenzo were new to the group.

Sam who was now talking to Lorenzo, he noticed, having looked her way without conscious thought.

"You better keep an eye on that boy. He's got the I-want-to-get-into-your-pants look written all over him."

"Lorenzo?" Clint asked. "Nah. He'll leave her alone."

"You think so?" Gigi asked. She sat on one of three logs near the fire, bent and picked up the potato peeler she'd set down on a cutting board. "Handsome girl like Sam," she said, using the sharp end of the utensil to rip into the bag of potatoes. "Of course he's making eyes at her."

"Does he know she's going blind?"

The words were out before he could call them back, and his grandmother's head jerked up. She narrowed her eyes, the peeler frozen in her hands. "So that's what this is all about," she said. "I had a feeling."

"A feeling about what?" he asked, glancing back at Sam and Lorenzo. The cowboy was smiling into Sam's face, and Sam was doing her best to smile back, but Clint could tell she wasn't in the mood.

"You're freaked out."

"Freaked out about what?" he huffed.

"Her going blind," Gigi said, exasperated.

"Of course I'm upset about that," Clint said. "I would have to have a heart of coal not to feel bad for her."

"You're falling in love with her."

"*What?*" he cried. "Don't be absurd. I just met the girl."

"Didn't stop you from jumping into her bed."

"I didn't jump into her bed."

Gigi raised her eyebrows before going back to her potato.

"All right, fine. Maybe I kissed her."

Her eyebrows swooped up again.

"A couple times," he added, but that was all he was going to admit. "That doesn't mean I'm in love with her."

Gigi scraped off a long strip of brown skin, one that she flicked into the fire. It hissed as it hit the flames. "I didn't say you were about to propose," she said, starting on another strip. "I said you were starting to care for her…before."

He wasn't going to ask "before" what because he got it. "I hardly know her, Gigi."

"Then why'd you give me the go-ahead to buy her expensive horse?"

"Because you were going to do it anyway, with or without me."

"True," she said, another peel going up in flames. "But you could have left me to my own devices. Instead you handed the lead rope to that horse over like a man handing his princess the keys to the castle."

"I did not," he said. "The transportation service guy did that."

Gigi stopped what she was doing. Her hands rested in her lap. "You wanted to do something nice for her," she said. "Not because it was the right thing to do—which it was, and we could afford it—but because you crossed the line. You went from feeling sorry for her to really, truly caring."

"Yeah?" he asked, shrugging his shoulders. "So what."

"And it scares the peanuts out of you that she's going blind."

He lifted his hat, swept his hair back with his hand. "No, it doesn't. I'm sure she'll be fine. Look how she's pulled through everything so far."

"Clinton, you lying sack of horse manure."

Cappie glanced up. Clint had a feeling the old army captain was listening to every word.

"You aren't just shrugging this off," Gigi said. "You're terrified for her. I can see it in your eyes, terrified because you'd started to fall in love with her."

"This is ridiculous," Clint said. "This isn't some damn Nicholas Sparks movie. People don't meet and fall in love in a matter of days. It takes months. If I look upset it's because now that I know she's going blind, I'm worried about how she's going to pay us back for Coaster."

His grandmother leaned back. "Wow," she said softly. "You really are in denial."

"I'm going to go check the horses."

"Just remember, Clinton," Gigi said, "Your grandfather used to bulldog cattle."

"Yeah? So?"

"He used to remind himself of something as he stared down the length of the arena. It wasn't the horse or the steer or his own damn head that would be responsible for him missing the horns, it was what was right here." She tapped her chest. "You gotta have heart. And you've got to let your heart lead you. If you do that, there isn't anything you can't do."

Terrific. She'd gone Obi-Wan Kenobi on him. Never a good sign.

"After I check the horses I'll go and get that bag of onions," he said. He'd noticed that Sam hadn't tied her horse up with the other ones. Probably smart. He was new to the barn and might get beat up being low in the pecking order.

He busied himself, checking saddles. Making sure all the packs were secure on the pack horses. Getting Gigi her bag of onions, then eating lunch when the time came. He noticed that Sam didn't eat, fought the urge to go over to her. Gigi would've beat him to it anyway. His grandmother brought Sam a plate, despite her protests.

Clint eyed the group. They were eight riders strong, each of the men necessary for the roundup. Four of them would herd the horses into the corrals. Another two would be left behind to work the gates of the corral. Another couple could ride the hills, searching for strays—although horses were herd animals and rarely left the pack. Still, a mare and foal could get lost, and they took great care to make sure no horse was left behind. After the animals had been vetted, sorted, microchipped and the males castrated, the wranglers would move them to higher pasture. Come summer, the lower hills would turn brown, but not the higher elevations.

The next day they'd do it all over again.

Point of fact it would take them a day to gather and work with the animals, and then another to move them to the higher pastures. The whole system was a matter of moving through one parcel, closing the gates, then moving them to another. Sort of like the Panama Canal.

Someone laughed.

Clint looked up. Lorenzo I-Want-to-Get-in-Your-Pants Villanueva was chuckling at something Sam was saying. This was his first year working with Clint and he could already tell it'd be his last. He didn't like the guy.

"Lorenzo," he called, "if you've got nothing better to do, maybe you can help Cappie pack up."

They were too far away for Clint to hear what Lorenzo said to Sam, but he would bet it was something sarcastic because Sam smiled. It set Clint's teeth on edge.

"Boys," he called, turning away from the two of them, "let's mount up."

He watched as the cowboys lounging on the ground scrambled up, plates in hand as they headed over to the chuckwagon. They looked like a posse of U.S. Marshalls, Clint thought. Something from the Old West. Most wore brown work shirts, all had chinks on, the leather fringe hanging down to just past their knees. Most had pocketknives tucked into the back of their jeans. The rifles they had were on their saddles, in a leather holder, but cowboy attire hadn't changed much in the past one hundred years or so.

"I want to make base camp tonight, so let's put a move on it."

Clint looked at Sam, about to offer to help her up, but Lorenzo—the little weasel—was already there. Hadn't he just told the guy to go help Cappie?

His mood didn't improve as they rode, Clint at the head of the pack. Their pace was slow because of the wagon they had to follow, but it was the perfect speed for chatting—which Lorenzo did. The kid kept trying to tease smiles out of Sam. Occasionally he'd succeed.

You're falling in love with her.

Damn, fool thing to say. As if he could fall in love with someone so quickly. Yeah, he felt sorry for her. Who wouldn't? But *fall in love?*

The idea made him so angry, he aimed his horse toward the chuckwagon, saying to Cappie and Gigi, "I'm going to ride ahead…make sure the trail's clear." Although he knew perfectly well it was. "I'll be back in a little while."

By tonight they'd be at base camp. If they were lucky, they might be able to spot one of the herds of mustangs, the ones that lived closest to the base camp.

Sam would like that.

He scrubbed a hand over his face. Sam again. He couldn't get the woman off his mind. At least that horse of hers was behaving. So far, the big gelding hadn't given anything a look. Not even the chuckwagon. But from what he knew of show animals, that shouldn't come as a shock. At the bigger shows, horses could see any number of things outside the arena because most of the time they were held at fairgrounds where just about anything could be going on at the same time. Car races, carnival rides, home improvement shows. More than likely, her horse was bombproof by now.

Maybe he was worth the twenty grand they'd paid for him.

And there he was, thinking about her blindness again. Gigi was right. It killed him. No one should have to face such a thing, least of all someone who'd already been through so much.

He rode as far as he could without losing sight of their group. It wasn't very far. Along the way he'd open and close gates for the crew. They'd hit the tree line. Tall oaks, aspens and cottonwood trees began to sprout up in more abundance. He stopped occasionally to glance back. Buttercup would toss his head as if contemplating a strafing run back to the others. Clint wouldn't let him. He'd turn and ride farther, the ten-foot wide path they followed marked by twin ruts. Evidence of their twice yearly trek into the hills.

During one of his stops, he noticed that Sam had broken away from the group. It was nearly the end of the ride, the sun having started to sink behind the trees. They were traversing some steep terrain now. Not so tight that they had to worry about the wagon sliding back down the hill, but tight enough that it was obvious they were at a new elevation. Sam continued to make her way toward him. Clint thought about riding ahead again. He'd leave her behind if he spurred his horse into a lope. But that would be irresponsible. He needed to keep an eye on the group. Plus, there was no reason to hide. And at least she was away from that damn Lorenzo.

"Hey," she said softly as she brought Coaster even with his horse.

"Hey," he said right back.

They were less than a half hour out from base camp and, frankly, she'd picked a good time to ride ahead. There was a spot farther up where the trees parted, they might be able to catch their first glimpse of the mustangs. This time of year, they liked to graze in a small valley.

"Gigi said I might be able to see the horses shortly."

Ah. That explained why she'd ridden up. Not to see him. Or to get away from Lorenzo. She wanted to see the horses.

Do you blame her, Clint? She'll never get to see them again.

"Yeah," he said, his throat tight all of a sudden.

"If we catch sight of them," she asked, her face more animated than it'd been all day, "will they be able to see us?"

He nodded. "A lot of times horses in our group will neigh to them. But they're used to our comings and goings. Sometimes in a dry summer even the upper pastures get low on grass and we have to supplement with hay. They don't consider us a threat, not once they realize we're not predators."

Sam nodded, her face in profile as she looked straight ahead—almost as if she was trying to catch an early glimpse of the break in the trees.

That's exactly what she's doing, moron. She probably doesn't want to miss a second.

"And if they're not in this valley, then what? Will we see them when we get to base camp?"

He shook his head. "If they're not in the valley it

means they're on the other side of yet another mountain. We'll have to ride over tomorrow. But it's not a long ride. Maybe an hour or so. We'll set off early."

She nodded again.

"You should see the valley we'll be camping in," he said. "It's—"

He couldn't talk. Abruptly, his throat tightened so that he couldn't force a word out of his mouth.

"What's wrong?" she asked.

"Nothing," he choked out. "As I was saying, it's really something else."

"You okay?" she asked, leaning forward so she could see beneath his cowboy hat. Aboard that monster horse of hers she was at least a foot above him.

"Fine," he said. "Should have taken a Benadryl before we left."

"I have some in my pack. I was thinking once we climbed higher my own allergies might act up, but, nope, I've been just fine. Of course, I've been so busy talking, I might just not have noticed. Lorenzo's been chatting my ear off. He's a nice guy. Did you know his ancestors were part of the Spanish land grant? Apparently his great-great-grandfather was some kind of Spanish noble…"

She was babbling, and he knew why.

She was giddy.

Her eyes glowed like the wings of a butterfly. She held the reins tightly, as if she needed something to hold on to to keep herself planted in the saddle. Speaking of that saddle, she was wiggling in it—when she wasn't craning her neck so she could look up ahead. If she'd asked him, he would have told her they were almost there. He could see the branches getting thinner. And there was the fallen oak, its broken trunk scarred by lightning.

"Sam," he said.

"…but I was thinking if we didn't see them tonight, maybe I could head out on my own—"

"Sam," he said again, louder.

"What?"

"Look." He pointed ahead.

Like drapes made out of foliage, the canopy of leaves parted. At first you could see nothing more than the mountain on the other side. But as they stepped closer, you could see more and more of the floor below, specifically, a lake about a mile below them, one surrounded by a treeless, grass-laden valley, and at the farthest edge of the water…

Sam gasped.

Clint knew she'd spotted them. The horses were exactly where he'd hoped they'd be—by the edge of the lake—their reflection shining up to them in the surface of the water. He was glad he sat next to Sam when she saw them for the first time.

"Oh, Clint." She pulled Coaster up. "They're so beautiful."

So was she. More beautiful in those seconds than any other woman he'd seen before. Tears filled her eyes, and he had to look away because if he didn't, she'd be in on his secret.

He was blinking back tears, too.

Chapter Eighteen

Sam didn't want to breathe she was so afraid of startling the horses below them. Coaster shifted beneath her, his ears suddenly pricked forward. He'd spotted them, too.

"Aren't they amazing, boy," she told her horse, patting him.

She'd seen wild horses on TV. Heck, she'd watched every horse documentary there ever was. But seeing them now, live, in the flesh, took her breath away. They were a distance away, if she held up her hand they'd be about the size of her thumbnail. They came in all different colors: bays, sorrels, black and gray. Sometimes all those colors were on one body, sometimes like Buttercup next to her, dappled.

Behind her, she could hear the wagon coming. One of their horses neighed. A second later, a few of the horses in the valley pricked their own ears. One of them—a black-and-white paint—trotted forward a few steps. He seemed to sniff the air, all the while looking in their direction. She watched as his tail rose up—like a flag of warning—his head climbing higher and higher as he tested the wind. And then he trotted forward again, only that trot turned into a gallop. All the horses in the band were looking in their direction now. The black-

and-white shook its head, his mane flying, and Sam knew this was the stallion.

"They're going to run," Clint said, his voice barely audible—as if he was afraid the horses might hear him.

"To where?" she asked.

"Not far. The end of the valley, probably. Like I said, they're not afraid of us. Once Atlas realizes we're not a herd of mountain lions, he'll settle down."

"Atlas?"

He looked up at her, nodded. "The black blotches of color. They look like continents on his sides."

She laughed. She couldn't seem to stop herself.

Mom, are you seeing this? They're real. Tomorrow I might even get to touch one.

"You two going to get a move on?" someone yelled. Cappie, Sam realized. The old coot had been giving her dark looks since the moment she'd gone to throw her plate away. She'd only nibbled at her hamburger and Cappie had seemed to take that as a personal affront.

"We're moving, we're moving," Clint said.

A few of the other riders rode ahead of the wagon.

"They down there?" Dean asked.

"They are," Clint answered.

Dean's horse neighed. Down below, the group of horses was coming to a slow stop. The black-and-white stallion—Atlas—had turned back to face them.

"I see he's still ruling the roost," Dean said.

"Is that the stallion?" someone else said. Lorenzo. "The black-and-white toby?"

Toby. Short for tobiano, a word used to describe the unique markings on the horse's body.

"That's him," Clint said.

Lorenzo reached around behind him, opened the duffel bag strapped to the back of his saddle and pulled out—

"Hey," Clint cried, whipping Buttercup around. "No cameras."

Sam didn't know how he reached the man so fast, but one minute the camera was in Lorenzo's hands, the next it was on the ground. Cappie and Gigi had caught up to them by then, Cappie's "Whoa" clearly audible.

"Hey!" Lorenzo said. "That's a three-hundred-dollar digital."

"I don't care if it's the Hubble Telescope. You were told before you came out here no cameras."

"Yeah, but those could be any wild horses in the world. What's the big secret?"

Clint leaned toward the cowboy. "You know damn well and good." He faced Gigi. "We made a mistake bringing this kid along." He turned Buttercup toward another one of the wranglers, a dark-haired man Sam had been introduced to, but whose name she couldn't remember. "Craig, escort Mr. Villanueva back to the ranch, would you."

"Hey, man," Lorenzo said, "you don't have to send me back. I'm sorry. I won't do it again."

"Not good enough," Clint said, swinging a leg over the front of his saddle and sliding off like it was a lounge chair. He picked up the camera. "You're going back, and I'm keeping this."

"You can't do that."

"Watch me."

"Clint," Gigi said. "Don't be so hard on the kid. He made a mistake, that's all."

"I don't care. I want him off my ranch. Now."

"And I want my camera."

"No."

"It's worth a lot of money," Lorenzo said.

"I'll reimburse you for it."

Lorenzo looked at Gigi as if hoping she might take his side again. She didn't.

"Come on," Craig said, adjusting the cowboy hat on his head. "Let's get started down the hill. We have to make it to the camp before sundown."

Lorenzo glanced in her direction next. Sam just shook her head. The idiot should have known better.

"Go," Clint all but yelled.

Lorenzo jerked on the reins, and Sam winced. She could tell he'd hurt his horse's mouth.

"Damn fool," Clint said, bending and picking up Buttercup's reins.

No one said a word.

"He's lucky I didn't knock him off his horse."

Gigi cleared her throat, eyes on her grandson. "Me thinks the man doth protest too much."

Clint swung back to her, the heel of his left boot digging into the ground. "Aw, what the hell is that supposed to mean?" he asked, wrapping the strap of the camera around his wrist.

"Nothing," Gigi said, all innocence.

Sam looked between the two. She wasn't the only one to stare at them. Obviously there was more to this conversation than met the eye.

"Let's go, everyone," Clint said, stuffing the camera in his pack. He didn't even use the stirrup when he swung up onto his horse, something Sam had always wished she could learn to do. 'Course, Clint's horse wasn't seventeen-plus hands.

They rode off, the jingle of the chuckwagon's harness following in their wake. Nothing could have spoiled Sam's mood. Not Clint's standoffish behavior earlier, not the altercation with Lorenzo, nothing. She'd seen the horses. Finally.

Their base camp was at the foot of the same mountain they'd just traversed, at one end of a long valley. Sam could tell in an instant that the Baer family had been there many, many times before. There were logs surrounding the sleeping area, their trunks long since stripped of branches and bark, the wood beneath it the dark gray of a silver fox. A blackened area of earth marked where countless fires had been. The shore of the lake wasn't far away, either, nor the line of trees they'd just emerged from. It was like an oasis in the hills.

"There's horse pens over there," Clint said, pointing. Sam turned. To her left the mountains formed a V. A long time ago, someone had built a massive corral, the boards blending in with the surroundings to the point that she hadn't noticed it at first. On purpose, she realized. The neutral material camouflaged the chutes in such a way that the wild horses probably wouldn't see them until the last minute, making them easier to catch.

"You can put Coaster in one of them," Clint added. "Unless you think he'll be okay in with the other horses."

She almost reminded him that Coaster was technically his horse, but she didn't want to do that. Not when his mood seemed to be improving by the minute. Maybe he'd just been stressed about getting to camp. Maybe that's why he'd spent the better part of a day ignoring her.

"I'd rather keep him separate," she said. "At least until he gets used to the other horses."

Clint nodded, but his attention was quickly taken by one of the cowhands. Left to her own devices, Sam made quick work of stripping the tack off Coaster so she could turn him loose in one of the handful of pens that lined the corral.

"You were a doll today," she told the horse, giving him a pat before turning back to camp.

"What can I do to help?" she asked Gigi.

Gigi smiled. "You know, I love a person who's not afraid of work. Go on into the back of the wagon. We'll need help moving the bags of horse feed. There's a collapsible cart in there you can use to move them around."

That was the start of about an hour's worth of work. Each bag needed to be ripped open and a bucket of alfalfa cubes scooped out and fed to each horse. Fortunately, rain-fed water troughs were already filled because for a moment Sam had worried about having to lug water from the lake.

By the time everything was unpacked, the tents set up and the horses settled, it was nearing sunset. Sam dreaded the thought of doing this all over again in another location two days from now when they went after the second group of mustangs.

"Oh, dear me, no," Gigi said, her gray hair picking up the sun's waning rays so that it looked like liquid silver. "This is base camp. The three herds of mustangs we manage all live within a few miles of here. This herd actually lives in the same pasture as our corrals— here." She pointed to the ground. "The other two live through various gates to the north and south of us. We'll close off this one in the back pasture when we bring the other two herds for sorting and vetting."

"So the horses will stay in the same corral for the next week?" For some reason she'd been under the impression they'd be moving camp every night.

Gigi nodded. "Someone will bring fresh supplies for us this weekend, but we're putting down stakes right here."

"Wow," Sam said. It all seemed simple. She'd had it in her head that it'd be a convoluted mess to get up and gather three herds of horses. Instead it sounded like the hard part would be going out and finding them.

She lifted her hand to her eyes to look out across the lake.

And couldn't breathe.

Had her field of vision shrunk?

It was hard to say, but she knew of one surefire way to tell. She'd gotten good at perfecting the maneuver. Pulse pounding, she lifted her thumb, bringing it up to her line of sight. In that way she could gauge the amount of space between the edge of her nail and the area she was blind.

It had narrowed; no doubt about it.

The breath left her. What did this mean? It had narrowed a lot, and so quickly. Always before it'd been so slow as to be barely noticeable.

Okay, no need to panic, she told herself. She would check tomorrow, try to gauge how quickly it was shrinking. If at all. It might not shrink again for days, maybe weeks, with luck, months.

She tipped her head up. If that wasn't the case she would cross that bridge when she came to it.

SHE LOOKED SAD. Staring at the horses across the lake, Clint would have thought she'd be excited.

"Go to her, Clint," Gigi said, walking up and placing a hand on his shoulder. "She needs you."

"I don't know if I can," he admitted.

"Can what?" she asked.

"Be there for her," he said, glancing down at his grandmother. "You were right earlier, I've started to…" He shook his head. "I really care for her."

"Of course you do," Gigi said softly. "You wouldn't be the man you are today if you didn't have a great capacity for love."

"I didn't say I was in love with her."

She gave him a smile that said…*yet.*

He just shook his head again. This was when he either backed off or moved forward, eyes wide-open.

What a stupid analogy to use.

"I'll be right back," he said.

Gigi's smile was nearly as bright as the moon beginning to rise. It hung in the blue sky to her right. "Take your time. Dinner won't be ready for another few minutes yet. Tell her you understand."

He didn't understand, though. There was no way to ever comprehend what she must be feeling right now.

But he sure as hell wanted to try.

Chapter Nineteen

"You want to get closer?"

Sam jumped. "Can we?" she asked, looking up at him. Her butt had grown cold sitting there by the edge of the lake.

"Sure," he said, glancing over at his grandmother. "Dinner won't be ready for a while. We have some time. We just have to go above the tree line. Try and stay downwind of them. Come on. I'll take you there."

Sam's spirits lifted when he held out his hand. She stared at his fingers in question, wondering what he wanted until it suddenly dawned on her that he was simply trying to take her hand.

She smiled, and placed hers in his.

"Clint-and-Sam-kissing-in-a—"

Sam heard the thud of a hand connecting with flesh from where she stood.

"Oww," someone cried.

They both turned in time to see Dean clutching his midsection. "I was just teasing," he said to Elliot.

The old cowboy was whittling a piece of wood. "That'll teach you to open your mouth," the man said, absolutely deadpan.

Sam looked back at Clint and started laughing. He

smiled, too, but only after staring at her intently for a moment.

"Come on," he said, squeezing her hand.

He led her to the tree line, where the two of them had to climb before they were far enough into the trees that the horses wouldn't spot them. The brush was thicker here, Clint guided her along an animal trail. Above them, branches stretched toward the darkening sky. They had to duck those branches from time to time, and as they neared the end of the lake, Clint motioned with a finger that she should be quiet.

Her pulse quickened.

She knew they were close, could hear their soft snorts through the trees. One of them stomped a hoof—probably a fly on its leg. And then the two of them began to slowly move down the hill, through the trees and shrubs, Clint motioning her behind him. They moved silently, stealthily until, at last, the trees began to thin again and there—right there—not more than fifty feet away, was a buckskin mare, her black tail so long it dragged on the ground. Clint stopped at the trunk of a tree and they squatted to watch.

Thirty or so head grazed peacefully in front of them.

Oh, Clint.

She didn't say the words—of course she didn't—but she told him with her eyes. They hadn't been spotted yet... Around back of the mare a colt with big brown eyes peered in their direction, ears pricked forward, then shifting back, then forward again. Had it caught their scent?

She shared a grin with Clint. The old Clint. Not the surly, standoffish man who'd taken his place for the past twenty-four hours.

Hooves thundered. Atlas was running toward them.

Had the big stallion spotted them? If he had, what would he do? The horse paused by the edge of the clearing, nostrils flaring.

Atlas had their scent. Clint slowly stood as Atlas's head lifted. Sam tensed, wondering if the stallion would come at them, teeth bared. But Clint had been raised around this horse, she realized, he must know what it would or would not do. Sure enough, Atlas wheeled around, the mares nearest to him shying away. In a second they were all running, the tiny baby horse Sam had been laughing over squealing and trailing in its mother's wake.

"That was incredible," Sam said as she also stood, her hand at her chest. "I mean, just incredible. I will never, ever forget that."

"Never?" he asked.

She faced him, the thing that always danced through the air whenever they were together returning.

"Never."

"Sam," he said, his eyes more blue than she'd ever seen them. It must be the backdrop of the lake. Or the sky, which was changing from blue to purple to deep, vivid orange near the mountaintops. "I think I owe you an apology."

"No," she said softly. "You don't, Clint."

"Yes, I do," he said. "I couldn't deal with it, not at first."

"Deal with what?"

"Your going blind," he admitted.

"Yes," she said. "I am. But it's not like I'm dying. I don't have a terminal disease, Clint. I'm going blind, and that terrifies me, but I'll make it through."

He didn't say anything. Sam's pulse picked up with each second of silence.

"You amaze me," he said at last.

"And you amaze me," she said. "You bought a horse, sight unseen, from some crazy woman who showed up on your doorstep...all because you felt sorry for her. Excuse me, but I'm not the amazing one here."

He captured her hand. "Shh," he said, and then he was kissing her and Sam was grateful—oh, so grateful—that he'd gotten over his fears, or his anxiety, or whatever it was that had upset him about her going blind. When Clint kissed her, she forgot all about her troubles, all there was in the world was Clint.

"Eeooooow."

The sound echoed across the lake, and Clint and Sam pulled apart. A lazy stream of smoke marked the location of the base camp. They'd been so busy staring at the horses they hadn't noticed the break in the trees, the one that allowed base camp a perfect view of them.

"Dean," Clint identified. They could just make the kid out at the edge of the lake. And if they could see *him*, he could see *them*. "Come on."

"Where are we going?"

"Someplace nearby," Clint said.

"Is it a cabin?"

He laughed, shook his head. "I wish. But it's a place I used to go to as a kid. My mother used to call it a fairy ring. It's a clearing in the trees."

A few seconds later she found herself asking, "Do you miss her?"

It took Clint a second to follow the direction of her thoughts. All he could think about was getting Sam someplace where they could be alone, where he could kiss her again, make her cry out and...

"Yes," he said. "I miss her every day of my life."

He saw her nod. "I miss my mom, too. And my dad,

of course, but especially my mom. I wish she could have been with us today."

"She is," Clint said, smiling at her. "She is."

Her tender smile made Clint ache with need. She was so beautiful, her skin such a flawless, ivory color that he doubted it'd ever been marred by a blemish for Sam's entire life.

"There," he said, recognizing a spot not far ahead. It was the only place in the forest where ferns grew, something Clint had often wondered about in the past. Why here? And why were they so thick? He didn't know, but what was more remarkable was the way the ground flattened out, the way they could step through the thick foliage and then emerge in the middle of a small clearing, one with soft sprigs of grass.

"Amazing," he heard Sam mutter.

No. What was remarkable was the wonder in her face.

"Come here," he said.

She needed no second urging.

They met as they had on that first night, quickly, greedily, his mouth covering her own with such force that she opened for him immediately.

Yes.

This was what he wanted. To taste her, to let his tongue glide across hers.

He pulled back, looked into her face and tried to tell her what he was feeling with his eyes.

"I know," she said, reading his mind. "I feel the same way."

His fingers worked the buttons of her denim shirt. She did the same, the both of them knowing this was the moment. Out in the open, with the Baer Mountain Mustangs grazing not far away, and Mother Nature providing the bed.

That seemed right.

Not even Julia had been here, Clint thought. Oh, he'd invited her on a roundup, but she'd declined. She'd never even wanted to see the horses.

"I feel like a teenager," Sam said, peeling his shirt off his shoulders.

Thank God he'd never married Julia. "Me, too," he said, doing the same to Sam. "I feel like we're about to do it in the back of a car."

"Yeah, but this is so much better," she said, her hands on the waistband of his jeans.

"I don't have a condom," he admitted.

"If you carried one I'd be worried." She smiled up at him impishly. "And offended."

The snap of his jeans popped free. It amazed him how just that one sound had him growing hard. He'd been aroused since he'd kissed her, but the knowledge that he was about to be held by her, stroked by her—man— it turned his insides out.

"Sam," he said.

She reached a hand inside.

Clint gasped. Her fingers were warm and she knew exactly how to touch him. One long stroke was all it took to get him to sigh, and when those same fingers slipped beneath the elastic of his boxers, he gasped.

"You're going to be the death of me," he muttered.

"Yes," she said, "but what a way to die."

He couldn't dispute that, didn't have any breath left in him to do anything more than moan when her fingers wrapped around his bare flesh.

"I'm going to do to you exactly what you did to me," she said, sliding down his body.

No, he wanted to say. *Let me take the rest of your clothes off, lay you down on a bed of grass, part your legs.*

Her mouth found him.

He cried out. She stroked him. He meant to stop her. He truly did, but when he opened his eyes and saw her kneeling there, he realized he was a lost man. He moaned again even though it was greedy of him to let her continue. But he couldn't seem to stop watching her.

"Sam." He was about to lose it.

Clint saw spots dance before his eyes. Only by sheer force of will did he pull back. But she must have seen how close he was because she took him again—

"Sam." He pulled back. "Not yet." He wanted to prolong their time together. He wanted to remember each and every little detail.

He quickly got rid of his boots and jeans, standing in front of her naked. He knelt before she could get any ideas, his hands finishing the last of her buttons before starting on her jeans. Thankfully they had a zipper fly.

"I want to taste you again," she said, her green eyes never leaving his.

"And I want to taste you," he said, leaning her back.

"Clint, no—" But she lifted her hips. Clint used it as an opportunity to jerk her jeans away. He forgot about her boots, made quick work of tugging them off. In seconds she was naked, too, and he was hovering between her legs.

"Yes," she sighed, lifting her hips again.

"Glutton," he teased, but he needed no second urging. She cried out when he made contact, her whole body jerking. His tongue elicited the same sounds out of *her* as she'd teased out of *him.*

"Yes," she cried. "Oh, Clint. Just like that. Don't. Stop…."

Only she was quicker to climax for him this time than before and he wondered if she'd been fantasizing about him on the long ride over.

"My turn," he said, moving up her body.

Clint paused to memorize her expression of satisfaction. And then he had to force himself not to shut his eyes as he glided into her silky middle.

"Sam," he moaned, taking things slow at first, though what he wanted to do was plunge inside her, hard, and then plunge again.

She took matters into her own hands, thrust herself up to greet him, telling him without words that she wanted it as hard as he could give it to her, and as fast.

He drove himself home, stared into her eyes.

Their two gazes locked as he rode her harder.

"Clint," she cried just before she arched her head back and cried out. He felt her body pulse around him, knew she'd climaxed again. He thrust inside her one more time and then it was his turn to fly.

"Clint," she moaned, matching his every thrust. "Oh, Clint."

Her spasms subsided, but his own pleasure rolled on. "I'm going to take care of you," he murmured, holding her tight. She trembled in his arms. "You don't ever have to worry, Sam." He clutched her to him and then rolled her on top of him. "I promise, Sam. I'll be there for you. Through thick and thin. Always. You don't ever have to worry," he said again and again.

He meant every word. Sam knew that. She just wished he didn't make it sound like she needed taking care of. She didn't.

She'd be fine.

Chapter Twenty

Clint insisted Gigi would know something was up if they didn't return to camp right away. But as they made their way back, Sam couldn't keep a smile off her face. The sun was behind the mountains now, the valley in shadow. It was stunning, the mercury color of the sky reflected in the smooth surface of the lake. Clint held her hand, and she couldn't ever remember being happier.

I wish you could have met him, Mom and Dad.

"There you two are!" Gigi gushed as she and Clint walked into camp hand in hand. "I was starting to worry about you."

"No need. I was keeping a sharp eye on her," he said, smiling down at her. Sam squeezed his hand.

"I'll bet," Gigi said. "But dinner's ready. Better eat before it gets dark so you can see your food."

"Nah," Clint said. "That's what campfires are for."

"Go," Gigi said, and Sam had the feeling if she'd had a dish towel she'd have whipped Clint on the rear with it.

For the rest of the night, he kept her company. The sky darkened. Someone stoked the fire. Clint pulled her to his side and they talked. For hours. They shared tales from their childhood, horse stories, work stories, and as they talked, Sam realized she could fall in love with this man. Heck, she was probably more than halfway there already.

Gigi left them alone, as did the wranglers. But before Clint's grandmother went to bed, she wished them goodnight, the firelight reflected in her teeth as she grinned.

"She knows," Sam said.

"Of course she does. Gigi doesn't miss a thing."

"Do you think she minds?" Sam asked, looking up at him.

He shook his head. "Are you kidding? This is all part of her master plan. I wouldn't have put it past her to have orchestrated this whole thing."

He kissed her in front of everybody, and Sam kissed him back. It amazed her how instantly her body flared to life. It was as if he knew instinctively how to touch her. Or maybe it had to do with body chemistry. Whatever the case, when Clint touched her, she melted in his arms like caramel on a hot summer day. Later, much later, he grabbed two bedrolls, and, feeling like a teenager, Sam let Clint take her hand. He led her into the woods where they made love a second time.

Sam woke up the next morning in Clint's arms.

"Good morning," he said, smiling down at her.

Sam stretched. Surprisingly, she wasn't all that sore. Must have been the aspirin she'd taken. "What time is it?" she asked because the sky was still dark. Not inky-black, but the blue-gray of a sky about to be invaded by the sun.

"It's time to get up," he said, kissing her lightly.

"I think someone already is up," she murmured against his mouth.

"Yeah, but that'll have to wait."

She knew he was right. Today would be a busy day. Today she would herd wild mustangs.

Her heart began to beat harder at the thought of it.

When Clint wasn't looking she closed one eye and then the other and tried to gauge if her field of vision had shrunk any more.

It hadn't.

She breathed a sigh of relief. Perhaps it'd been a one-time change. Perhaps she had nothing to worry about. A few more weeks, maybe a month or so, that's all she asked. She wanted to get to know Clint while she still had her sight. Of course, they hadn't talked about where their relationship was going, but they would. After last night it was obvious there was something between them, something wonderful and miraculous that couldn't be denied.

"Let's go," Clint said after they both dressed.

The camp was just starting to stir when they arrived. Cappie and Gigi were already up, and Clint's grandmother raised an eyebrow when she spotted them sneaking back. Sam smiled sheepishly and went to go feed the horses.

Less than an hour later they were off. Sam couldn't keep the smile off her face as they headed out. Coaster seemed to sense her excitement. He tossed his head. She clutched the reins, stroked his mane. "Easy, boy."

"What's the matter?" Clint asked. "Is he okay?"

"He's fine," she said, glancing down at him. "He's just excited. As am I."

"But he's never been on a roundup before. We have no clue how he'll react to a group of horses galloping next to him."

"He'll be fine," Sam said again. "Relax, Clint. I've had Coaster since he was a foal. We know each other like the back of our hands…or hooves, as the case may be. Coaster's about as laid-back as a horse can be. I doubt he'll do more than toss his head today."

Clint didn't look convinced. Sam just shook her head. He'd understand sooner or later.

They rode a different path than the one they had taken yesterday. They didn't ride alongside the lake or back up the hill. Instead they headed away from the mustangs, following a tiny creek sandwiched between two mountains. They would give the wild horses a wide berth, she'd been told, through the trees to camouflage the wranglers' approach and get behind the horses. They wouldn't wave their hats or yell *yee-haw.* This wasn't the movies. Instead they would slowly encroach upon the mustangs' space, urging them forward. Once they were moving in the direction they wanted, they would push the animals toward the corrals where Dean and one of the other wranglers waited to help guide them in.

"Gosh, this is so beautiful," she said. Trees formed a shelter over their heads, their leaves bright green in the rising sun. The creek gurgled peacefully. That, combined with the sound of the horses' hooves, formed a rhythmic lull that made Sam think life couldn't get any better.

Thank God I survived that accident. I was meant to see this.

She believed the words with every fiber of her being, but there was something deeper going on. She sensed her mom here. It was almost as if she rode along with them.

They followed a path that looked to have been widened by horses' hooves over the years. She could see evidence of their passing in the mud alongside the water.

"Careful of that tree," Clint said.

"I see it." Sam glanced down at him again. "You don't have to babysit me. Coaster and I will be fine."

"Just the same, I'd feel better if you stuck by my side."

That hadn't been the case yesterday. She almost reminded him of that fact. They were making quick progress. She would bet they'd be upon the herd of mustangs within minutes.

Sure enough, Clint said, "We're going to turn off the path here in a second. I want you to hang back just in case Coaster gives you trouble."

Hang back? But Clint was the boss and she knew he had her best interest at heart.

Her palms were sweaty. She could feel the perspiration between her fingers. And her heart beat so hard she could feel it throb in her neck. This was it…she was about to round up mustangs!

"Okay, guys!" Clint called. "Let's do this nice and slow."

That must be why it was anticlimactic. They began walking down a slight slope, Sam at the back of the pack, much to her disappointment. In a matter of minutes they were out of the trees, and the horses in the valley were swiveling to face them. Atlas broke free, the big stallion trotting a few steps toward them before he skidded to a stop and tossed his head.

Sam smiled.

It was almost as if the horse was signaling for them to stop. Clint and the boys just kept coming. Atlas ran a ways toward them. Sam watched as Clint—who was in the lead—took off his hat and waved it. Atlas turned. Immediately, he began to gather his heard, the mares and foals clumping together near the middle as Atlas continued to keep a wary eye on them. When they were two hundred yards away, he apparently had had enough. He nipped at the rear end of the mare closest to him. She darted away, headed toward the right side of the lake. He bit another mare. Soon, the entire herd was on the move. The lead mare—a flashy-looking palomino— broke into a trot.

The butterflies in Sam's stomach began to flutter in earnest.

She'd been warned the mustangs might run. Clint had been hoping they wouldn't, but soon the head mare loped off. And then a second mare did the same. And then the next instant they were galloping. They hugged the shoreline, Atlas bringing up the rear, Sam watching as Clint rode after them at a trot. But when the band of mustangs picked up more speed, he spurred his own horse into a run.

"Stay back," he called to her.

Yeah, yeah, yeah... The black gelding was being well behaved. All he did was prick his ears at the horses running. He didn't prance. Didn't lift his tail and try to run away with her. He just meekly broke into a trot and followed at a distance. "Well, this is bunk," she told him. "Clint gets to have all the fun."

As if her words prompted the mustangs into action, they kicked into high gear. Sam nearly laughed. Just what Clint didn't want. It would make slowing them down at the end of the valley difficult. Not only that, but when the mustangs found their usual path blocked, they'd try to turn back, which meant they would all have to work hard to keep them down at the right end of the valley.

"Come on, boy," Sam said. "Let's be ready."

Coaster seemed pleased to pick up the pace. His head was up, his short, show-length mane dancing in the wind as he cantered behind Clint and the other cowboys. They'd had to pick up the pace. It was either that or the herd would get too far away to control. She saw Clint lean forward a smidge, a sure sign that he was about to go even faster.

Sam could do nothing but smile. How did she get

here? How did she end up in the Baer Mountains chasing after their fabled mustangs? She cocked her head, catching a glimpse of herself in the surface of the lake. Coaster's tail streamed out behind him, his legs a blur on the water's smooth surface.

"Come on, Coaster," she said. "Let's go."

They ran. Flat out, balls to the wall, *ran*. The wind forced tears out of her eyes.

The mustangs were nearing camp. Sam could make out Dean up ahead, the wrangler waving a coiled rope in an attempt to keep the horses headed toward the corral. Opposite him, another wrangler did the same. But the palomino mare leading the pack must have sensed their impending capture because she turned, saw Dean, turned again…and headed right back for them.

Uh-oh.

But Clint and his cowboys anticipated the move. They fanned out so that when the rest of the herd dove right, they had them all blocked off. Well, almost all of them. The palomino pinned her ears, spotted an opening between Clint and another wrangler, and made a dive for it. Sam heard Clint curse.

She pulled up.

She might be able to block the mare's path if she timed things right. She'd have to back up a little, let the mare think she could slip between Coaster and the lake, then shut her off at the last second, driving her toward the water's edge. She'd stop for sure. Maybe even roll back.

She tensed as the mare approached. Clint would surely kill her for doing this, but she was positive she could help….

"Whoa!" she yelled in the mare's direction before recognizing how stupid that was. This horse didn't know the meaning of *whoa*. She would have to stop her the hard way.

"Get ready, Coaster," she told her horse because the mare was advancing fast. A glance toward base camp told her the rest of the horses had been contained. They were being pushed into the corral.

The sound of hooves grew louder and louder. Sam tensed. Coaster lifted his head. She took one hand off the reins and rested it against his neck. This would be a test of Coaster's abilities. Some horses didn't like it when another animal ran at them full tilt. However, Sam had spent countless hours at horse shows where horses were known to spin, slide stop or speed by at ninety miles per hour. In a nutshell, Coaster had seen it all. And so her wonderful show horse merely stood his ground, Sam clucking him forward when the palomino was about fifty feet away. The mare pinned her ears. Sam kicked Coaster into a trot.

"Sam!" someone yelled. She could tell it was Clint, but Sam was too busy to look.

"Whoa," she called again, but this time for Coaster's benefit. The mare skidded to a stop. For a split second, Sam thought the horse might dart around Coaster's back end. Instead she spun on her hind feet and turned back toward camp.

Perfect.

Sam couldn't contain her smile. She caught Clint's eye. He'd been riding toward her, but when he saw the mare headed his direction, he turned, too, giving the mare plenty of space to get back to her herd. It looked like most of the horses were in the corral, only a few stragglers hanging behind. Sam rode forward, intent on lending a hand.

"What the *hell* were you thinking?"

Chapter Twenty-One

Clint couldn't remember the last time he was so furious.

"What do you mean what was I thinking?" she asked, her mouth dropping open. "I was stopping that horse." She pulled Coaster to a halt.

"You could have been killed," he said, pulling up his own horse next to her.

"Clint, relax. I'm fine."

"Because you were *lucky,*" he said. Geez, his heart was still in his throat. "I told you to stay back."

"I *did* stay back. That's how I was able to help you."

"Well next time don't help," he said.

"Why?"

"Because you have no idea what you're doing. And with your eyes the way they are…"

Her face fell. "So that's what this is about?" she asked. "My eyes."

"Hell, yeah, it's about your eyes. You told me yourself you've lost peripheral vision. What if that horse had come at you wrong? What if she'd ducked into a blind spot? What then?"

"Coaster would have taken care of me," she said, lifting her chin.

"Coaster isn't even *your horse.*"

"True," she said slowly.

But he was already regretting the words. He scrubbed a hand over his face. He needed to shave. And out of nowhere the memory of him nuzzling the crook of her neck with his razor stubble came to him.

Shit.

"I'm sorry. I didn't mean that the way it sounded. I just lost my mind there for a second when I saw you dart in front of that horse. That's a move even my wranglers think twice about."

Her posture relaxed. "No, I understand. But I knew what I was doing. Heck, horses get loose at horse shows more often than you might think. It's not the first time I've had to head one off."

"Yeah, well, those horses have been taught to fear and respect humans. Not these mustangs."

She nodded. "I see your point." But she still looked upset.

His comment about Coaster must have stung more than he'd intended. "You know Coaster is yours, don't you?"

"No, Clint. He's not. He's yours. And Gigi's. You bought him. When my eyes give out, I'll have no way to repay you. Besides, when I get back home, what will I do with him?"

Clint glanced toward the corral. Dean had matters well in hand. The gates were already closed. Soon they'd start sifting through the herd. He needed to get back.

"You can keep him at our ranch," he said. "He can be your horse in all but name only, if that's what you want."

She shook her head. "That's not what I want. It's why I wanted to sell him in the first place." She reached down and stroked her horse's mane. "He should be shown. That's what he's good at. That's what he's trained to do."

Dean was looking in their direction. "We'll talk about this later," he said. "After we're done today."

"Sure."

"But do me a favor, would you?"

"What's that?"

"Hang back today. Don't go throwing yourself into the fray. Gigi loves that you're so quick to help, but today that could get you killed." He shifted in the saddle, gave his horse the cue to sidestep. "And I don't want anything happening to you," he said, catching her hand and tugging her toward him. That damn horse of hers was a giant and so she had to lean down. He kissed her, lightly, with just enough passion to remind her of all that they'd shared the night before. Then he released her and spurred his horse forward.

She hung back this time.

SAM COULDN'T STOP THINKING about their conversation. Sure there was the excitement of working with the horses—when she was allowed, which wasn't much— but frankly, she was given *too much* time to think. The most Clint let her do was help with the weanlings once they were sorted out, but, since there were less than ten babies, that was quick work. She asked if she could give the adult horses their inoculations. That was some-thing she gave to Coaster on an annual basis. But even though the horses were well contained in narrow, wooden chutes that were taller than all the horses, he still wouldn't allow her near. He was worried she'd get bitten. Or kicked. Or squished somehow—his words. It drove her nuts.

"Don't look so discouraged," Gigi said when they broke for lunch. Sam stood in the shade of the chuckwagon and stared into the corral at the wild horses milling about.

"He won't let me do anything."

Gigi smiled. "It's the way he was raised. My daughter, she married a McAlister, a ranching family just as steeped in tradition as the Baers. Clint gets that sexist cowboy attitude from both sides."

"It's driving me nuts."

"Better get used to it," Gigi said, patting her hand. "And cheer up. You could always help us serve food."

Sam shot Gigi a look, one meant to tell her—no offense—but that wasn't her cup of tea. She wanted to help with the horses. Now.

Of course, what she did instead was help Gigi out.

"Hang in there, kiddo," she said. "Clint might be a bit of a Neanderthal at times, but he doesn't mean anything by it. Just give him time."

The afternoon wore on, and as day slipped toward night, Sam knew they would have to talk. If she heard one more "Sam, stand back," she'd scream.

"Good work today," Clint said, coming up to her, his hair still wet from the quick dip he'd taken in the lake. "You handled those babies like a pro," he said, the denim shirt he wore left open so he could air-dry.

I am a pro, she wanted to say, but he was bending down, placing a quick kiss on her lips.

"Thanks," she said instead.

"When's dinner going to be ready?"

And, see, that annoyed her all over again.

"I have no clue," she said. "You'll have to ask Gigi."

A few of the other ranch hands trailed in his wake toward the chuckwagon. As it turned out, dinner was served just about immediately, Clint waving her over. Sam almost didn't eat. She honestly didn't know how she'd cope with his me-man, you-woman attitude.

"You look perturbed," he said, sitting next to her on one

of the logs encircling the camp. Sam had figured out they had been set in a circle to keep the wild horses out when they were being rounded up. "And you barely ate a thing."

As opposed to him. She'd watched him clean his plate of grilled trout and fresh vegetables. And then he'd gone back for more.

"I'm just not hungry," she said.

"Then we must need to work you harder."

It was still daylight out. The mustangs in the corral pawed and snorted, anxious to be free. After dinner, they'd release them back into the wild. Tomorrow they'd push them to a different pasture and then pick up the next band.

"Judging by how today went," she said, "I doubt I stand a chance of getting within two feet of those horses."

He held her gaze for a second before setting his plate down. "All right," he said, "let's have it out. What's on your mind?"

She stared at him head-on. "I just…" She tried to put into words how she felt. "I guess I just don't know how this is all going to work out."

He straightened. "What do you mean?"

"This," she said, motioning to the valley around them. "My eyes." And then, in a lower tone of voice because she was almost afraid to say the word aloud. "Us."

He took her hand. Sam was grateful for that.

"I told you last night," he said. "I'm going to take care of you."

"Not if 'taking care of me' means keeping me under lock and key."

"I don't do that."

"Yes, you do," she said. "Clint, you need to learn to relax. To let me help. I'm a good hand with horses. I might not be a professional trainer, but I've been riding for more than a few years. Please don't treat me like a child."

And hanging in the air between them were the words: *I might not get another chance at this.*

"I worry you'll get hurt," he admitted.

"I know," she said. "But that's my choice."

He nodded.

She took a deep breath and asked the question she'd been too scared to voice out loud. "What's going to happen when we're done here, Clint? Where will I go?"

"You can stay here."

It was what she'd wanted to hear, and yet…not. "I can't," she said. "I need to go back to Wilmington, to the Center for the Blind. I should prepare for what's going to happen. Now, while I can still see."

"You can do that here."

She shook her head. "No, I can't. I mean, I suppose I could," she quickly added. "But what about learning a new vocation? What about finding a job? I can't stay here with you and do nothing."

She wanted to. Oh, how she wanted to. But she wasn't going to do that. She refused to be a burden.

That's what'd been bugging her, she admitted. It wasn't Clint's overbearing attitude, although that played a part. Rather it was that she knew that somehow, someway, she needed to face the coming challenges on her own. Hiding out on the Baer family ranch wasn't an option, not if she wanted to keep some of her hard-won independence.

"I think I should go back to Delaware," she said.

His jaw dropped.

"Think about it, Clint," she said. "We've just met. I show up on your doorstep and suddenly you're buying my horse and offering me a place to live and telling me you'll take care of me. I appreciate that, I really do, but that's no way to start a relationship."

He looked out over the lake, and Sam thought he was easily the best-looking man she'd ever met. And here she was telling him she wanted to go away.

"I'm not saying I'll leave tomorrow," she said, clasping his hand. "I couldn't even if I wanted to. I'm just saying, maybe we should slow down a little, take some time for us *both* to contemplate what's ahead."

He released a sigh, or maybe it was more like a snort of disgust. "You are the most difficult, hardheaded, stubborn son of a gun I've ever met."

Funny, but that made her smile.

"I'm not going to pretend I like the thought of you leaving," he said. "Honestly, Sam, I've never felt this way toward a woman. Yeah, the thought of you going blind scares the hell out of me, but I'm willing to risk we can make it work out."

"I feel the same way," she said. "I think I'm falling in love with you," she said. "That seems impossible, but it's true, and *that* scares the hell out of me."

He placed a hand against the side of her face. "You don't ever have to be scared," he said. "Not *ever,* and not for *any* reason."

Chapter Twenty-Two

He held her that night.

Sam didn't know why she felt so anxious. Especially after they'd made love. When morning dawned, she was up before Clint. Ironically, she found herself at the chuckwagon, helping Gigi set up for breakfast. There were plates and forks and cups that needed to be put on the tailgate, their impromptu table. And coffee to be made and eggs to be scrambled.

"Mornin'," Clint said, coming up behind her and pulling her into his arms. She felt his chin on top of her head. "You ready to go chase some mustangs today?" he asked.

"Yeah," she said good-naturedly, trying to elbow him away. "If you'll actually let me chase some."

"Well, now, I can be bribed."

She whirled around. "You can?"

He nodded, his cowboy hat dipping low enough that for a second she couldn't see his eyes. "All you'd have to do is give me a kiss." He tapped his lips. "Right here."

"You mean it?"

"I mean it," he said. "And if you make it two kisses, I might just let you ride in the front with me."

She threw herself into his arms. He laughed, and then

she gave him not one, but five kisses. She might have given him more, too, but Dean started up his chant.

That was the beginning of one of the best days of Sam's life. Clint was as good as his word, letting her get right into the thick of things. She helped to push horses to higher ground, Coaster behaving like a perfect gentleman. After that, they set off after the next band. That took most of the morning. They broke for lunch. Afterward, they pushed the second herd toward the corrals. There were no wild mustang antics today, however, and the band of horses seemed to saunter down the hill and into the corral.

"That was easy," Sam said as they closed the gate.

"Not too bad," Clint agreed.

They started vetting the animals, Sam able to give shots this time. When Clint started to castrate the young colts, Sam realized she'd completely forgotten about his degree in veterinary medicine. There were a lot of horses to get through, though, and it quickly became obvious they'd have to finish up in the morning. But that was the plan. After so many years of caring for the bands of wild horses, Clint knew exactly how long it'd take to get the job done.

Another day passed. When Sam woke up in Clint's arms that third morning, she knew there was no place else she'd ever want to be.

They finished up with their second herd, moved them up to higher ground, too, then set off to find the final wild horses. This was the hardest part of the entire trip, Clint told her. The terrain they'd be crossing was steep and thick with trees. Sometimes it took them a while to find the animals; on one occasion they'd even had to give up, then come back and look for them another time.

Everyone was keeping a sharp eye out, peering between trees and studying the ground in hopes of finding evidence they were nearby. But they heard them before they saw them. In the distance, a horse neighed. A second one answered.

"This is our lucky day," Clint said to her with a smile.

"You want me to cut around?" Dean asked, riding up to them. It was his sorrel who'd neighed. "They must be in that bald spot up ahead."

"Yeah, they probably are. Why don't you and Elliot circle to the left. Sam and I will go right. You two stay here," he said to the remaining cowboys. "We'll drive them your way."

Everyone nodded and off they went, but because Sam's vision was impaired, she had to be careful riding through the low-hanging branches. She didn't tell Clint that, of course. The last thing she needed was for him to revert back to a caveman.

Honestly, it was ironic, really, because *she* was the one with the impaired vision and yet *she* was the one who spotted the man in the trees.

"Holy crap," she said, pointing. "There's a man up there."

Clint glanced over at her, puzzled. He followed her gaze. "Where?" he asked.

"There," she said. "He's wearing camouflage, but it's the wrong color. Brown. Look." She pointed.

The man—whoever he was—appeared to be focused on something directly in front of him.

"Holy—" Clint didn't finish his sentence. "It's that damn Lorenzo."

Lorenzo?

But she knew in an instant he was right, and that the cowhand had climbed a tree to use a camera he must've got to replace the one Clint had taken from him.

"Why that dirty little—" This time she didn't finish what she was going to say. She spurred Coaster after Clint who'd kicked his horse into a run.

Lorenzo must have heard them, because she saw him turn. She knew why his camouflage hadn't worked. The tree he was "hiding" in was full of lush foliage. His silly outfit stuck out like a bruise on an avocado.

"What the hell do you think you're doing?" Clint cried.

Sam winced. She'd heard that tone of voice before and it didn't bode well.

"Mr. McAlister," Lorenzo said, his gaze wide. Then he smiled, acting as if they hadn't just caught him up a tree on Baer Mountain with a camera in hand. "I…uh…I…"

Apparently, even the most brazen of idiots could be at a loss for words.

"Get down," Clint said.

Recognizing that he'd been caught red-handed, Lorenzo's expression changed. It amazed Sam that she'd ever thought he was handsome. He looked pure ugly now.

"I don't think so," he said.

"Get down or I'll pull you down."

"I'd like to see you try."

"Clint," one of the other wranglers called, obviously having spied them through the trees, "what's going on?"

"Nothing," he said. "Just dealing with some vermin."

"You need any help?" the guy asked.

"Nope." Clint's eyes never left Lorenzo as he un-strapped his rope.

"You wouldn't dare," Lorenzo said.

"Actually," Clint replied, uncoiling the rope, "I think I would."

Lorenzo leaped.

Sam gasped, the move so unexpected, even Coaster

jumped. The wiry cowboy landed on top of Clint like a stuntman in an old Western.

"Hey!" Clint cried.

"Son of a bitch." Lorenzo yelled.

And then they were falling, Sam recognizing that she was too close.

Sam watched in horror as the two men tumbled over backward. She tried to pull Coaster away, but there wasn't time. Clint and Lorenzo landed right at Coaster's feet. If she'd been a few paces away, it wouldn't have been a big deal, but even the most seasoned of cow horses would jump away from a pair of brawling humans.

She wasn't looking where Coaster was going, didn't have time to. And maybe if Sam's peripheral vision had been normal she might have seen the giant limb to her right. As it was, when Coaster ducked away, she didn't see it coming. One minute she was facing one way, the next there was a tree branch in front of her forehead.

"Clint!" she cried.

And then the branch hit her.

She was out cold.

Chapter Twenty-Three

"Sam!" Clint shoved Lorenzo off him and ran to her side. "Oh, my God, Sam."

He felt for a pulse. A vein throbbed beneath his finger. He breathed a sigh of relief, but it was only temporary. A bruise was already bubbling up purple on her forehead.

"Dean, Charlie, Elliot…anybody, call base camp."

Don't panic.

They had the radios for just this type of emergency. Walkie-talkies with a ten mile radius, and a two-way radio at the camp. Help could be here in a matter of minutes.

But help meant being airlifted out, and that could take up to a half hour to arrange.

Dean rode up. "What the hell."

"Use the radio," Clint said, not daring to leave Sam's side. "Tell Gigi what's happened. Tell her we'll need Life Flight. *And somebody find that damn Lorenzo.*"

Clint almost shooed Coaster away, but the big gelding was gingerly sniffing the human he loved as if trying to rouse her himself.

"It's okay," he said, though it was hard to decide who he said it to—Coaster or himself. "She'll be all right."

He heard yelling. The radio clicked. Voices buzzed. Clint remained focused on Sam. He kept stroking her hair, trying not to gag at the sight of that bruise—that horrible bruise.

"Hang in there," he told her.

It was taking too long. Too damn long.

The radio clicked again. Clint lost track of time. He kept feeling for her pulse, reassuring himself that she was alive, but her face had grown pale. Too pale.

"God." How had he not recognized that he was in love with her? Blind. Deaf. In a wheelchair, he didn't care. He loved her. "Come on, Sam. Wake up. Please," he begged.

He heard a thumping sound and looked up. Everybody stared down at him. He had no idea how long they'd all been standing there.

"They're landing in the clearing," Dean said. "Gonna bring a stretcher to her."

How long had he been kneeling there? Long enough for his knees to cramp and for Sam's face to turn waxy.

"How old is she?" someone in a flight suit asked the moment they reached Sam's side.

"I—" He didn't even know; he'd never asked her. "Twenty-five…I think."

The man nodded absently, his hands moving quickly as he pulled out a stethoscope, another man kneeling on the opposite side of him and pulling out a blood pressure cuff. Clint moved out of the way, swiveling around before forcing himself to look back. But there was no escaping the grim reality of the situation. Sam was hurt. Perhaps badly.

As badly as when her parents had died?

He drew a hand down his face, his eyes burning. No. It wouldn't be like before. That would be impossible.

"Let's get her on the backboard," one of the EMTs said. "Is someone going to meet her at the hospital?"

Clint nodded. "I'll meet her."

"Are you her husband?"

"No," he choked out. "Boyfriend."

"How long will it take you to get back to civilization?" the other man asked, blue eyes full of compassion.

"Half a day's hard ride," Clint said. "Can you take me with you?"

"Sorry, sir. Can't take anybody onboard but the immediate family."

"I understand," he said.

"We'll be taking her to St. Benedict's."

St. Benedict's. That was over an hour away…once he reached the ranch.

"All right," the guys said. "Let's get this done. People, you'll need to give us some space."

IT WAS THE LONGEST RIDE of Clint's life. Dean, Elliot and a few of the other guys all rode down the hill with him. By the time they arrived back at the ranch it was growing dark. Their horses were covered with sweat, their sides heaving, heads lowered as their nostrils flared in and out.

"Take him," Clint said to Dean, throwing him Buttercup's reins.

"Do you need us to go with you?" Dean asked.

"No," he called over his shoulder. He didn't want company. Not even Gigi, even if she hadn't still been at camp. Or maybe she was on her way down the hill, too. He hadn't stuck around long enough to find out.

"Let us know how she is!" Dean shouted after him because Clint was already on the move.

He didn't answer, just headed straight for his truck. His cell phone wasn't in there and so he had to run into the house to grab it, sweating every precious second. The minute he hopped into his truck he dialed Information. Again, he was made to wait. Clint pressed down on the accelerator as if that would make the operator on the other end speed up. When at last he did get through to the hospital, he was transferred three times, first to the E.R., then to Neurology—Clint's gut wrenched when he heard that—then back to E.R. When a doctor finally picked up the line, Clint wanted to cry out in relief. But his relief quickly changed to frustration. All the man told him was that she was in intensive care and they were running tests to determine the extent of her injuries. Best to get to the hospital as soon as possible.

"Damn it," he cursed as he hung up.

He drove like a maniac. St. Benedict's was past Billings. He had to go through town to get there. Traffic clogged the roads, or at least it felt that way to Clint. It was dark by now, the red points of light that stopped him a constant source of frustration.

God, keep her alive.

"Come on," he told the car in front of him, banging on the steering wheel. When he finally arrived at the hospital, he was in such a hurry he didn't even bother to park, just pulled to a stop alongside the E.R.'s loading zone and jumped out.

"Sir," one of the hospital volunteers called, "you can't park there."

"Tow it," he told the man.

"Samantha Davies," he said to the receptionist. "She came in on a Life Flight hours ago."

"Spell the last name for me?" The woman had bright red hair and too much lipstick and she appeared entirely bored with her job.

"Davies," Clint said. *"D-A-V-I-E-S." Hurry up.* Sam was injured somewhere in this hospital…she could already be…

He refused to think it.

"Ah, here she is," the woman said. "She's in Intensive Care. That's in the basement. Elevator to your right—"

But he was already on the move. He pressed the button with more force than necessary, and when the elevator doors didn't immediately open, looked around for stairs. He couldn't find any and so he spent what seemed like an eternity waiting. The door opened with a *bing*.

When at last he arrived at the Intensive Care desk, he was out of breath and scared to death. "Samantha Davies," Clint gasped.

"Are you family?"

Telling the Life Flight EMTs he wasn't Sam's husband had cost him a helicopter ride. "Yes. I'm her husband."

The woman stood. She looked too young to work in a place like this—younger than him. "Sit down over there," she said. "I'll page the doctor."

"Can't I see her?" he asked.

"Not yet. They're still running tests. She'll be in room 102 when they're finished."

Running tests. So she was still alive. Thank God. For a moment there when she'd told him she was going to page the doctor, he'd thought…

But it didn't matter what he thought. She was here. She was alive. More important, *he* was here. She wouldn't have to wake up in a hospital all alone again.

If she woke up.

Clint removed his hat, ran a hand through his hair and waited for the doctor. When he didn't appear right away, Clint checked in with the nurse. She just smiled and said he was on his way. On his way to where? Clint wanted to ask. The golf course?

"Mr. Davies?" a man finally asked.

Clint shot up from the blue plastic chair he'd been sitting on, nearly knocking the thing over. "That's me," he said without missing a beat.

"I'm Dr. Tyson," said a man who wasn't much older than Clint. He had dark hair and the pale skin of a man who spent too much time indoors, but his blue eyes projected kindness and reassurance. Clint appreciated that.

"Clint," he said, almost adding McAlister, but he caught himself.

"Your wife is very sick, Mr. Davies."

"How sick?" he asked, hardly able to breathe his heart beat so fast.

"She has some swelling of the brain—"

Shit. "Not again."

"Has she sustained this type of injury before?"

"Yes," he said. "A few months ago. Car accident."

"Did she completely recover from her injuries?"

"Yes…no," he quickly corrected, motioning toward his eyes. "She has an embolism. Near her central artery," he said because for the life of him he couldn't remember the name of the vein she'd told him.

"Ah," the doctor said. "That's good to know." He pulled a chart up, one Clint hadn't even noticed he'd been holding. "Unfortunately," he said, "that's the least of our concerns right now. She sustained a pretty hard blow to the head. There's some swelling…"

Clint barely heard the rest of the doctor's words. Really, there was only one question Clint wanted to ask. "Will she be all right?"

"We don't know yet. At this point, we need to see how she responds to the medication we've given her. If it helps to reduce the swelling, we might be in good shape. I say *might* because, as always, there's no prediction if she'll have any long-term damage. But you probably already know that having been through this before."

No. He hadn't been through this before, but he didn't tell the doctor that. "Is she in a room?"

"They're hooking her up to monitors as we speak. When they're done, you can go in, but I'll have to ask you to keep your visit short. There's going to be a lot of people in and out over the next few hours."

Clint nodded, sat down and waited some more, hat in hand. He was playing with it absently when a familiar voice said, "Where is she?"

Clint looked up, never more relieved than when he spotted Gigi. "They're setting up her room. She's in critical condition. Swelling of the brain."

"Oh, Clint."

And then somehow he was in Gigi's arms. She held him while he fought to control his emotions. He would not cry. He refused to cry. Crying meant weakness and he needed to be strong for Sam.

Stronger than he'd ever been before.

Chapter Twenty-Four

If he'd thought the long ride down the hill interminable, that was nothing compared to what Clint had to endure over the next few hours. He got to see Sam only briefly. But she was hooked up to so many devices it was hard to *see* her. He saw the tube down her throat—had been told it was there in case the swelling in her brain caused her to stop breathing. Right now she was in an induced coma. She would stay that way until they knew whether or not her brain would heal itself.

Gigi kept him company. Over the course of the night, Dean and Elliot showed up, too, then more and more of his ranch hands. It was a sweaty, grungy, motley-looking crew that waited for news.

It came at 9:00 the next morning.

"We're in good shape," the doctor said, coming into the waiting room. "The swelling's going down."

There were whoops from all the cowboys, but the doctor held up his hands, shushing them. "We still need to wait and see if her brain activity returns to normal."

"When will we know?" Clint asked.

"Too soon to say," Dr. Tyson said. "These things, sometimes they resolve in hours, sometimes days, sometimes weeks...sometimes never. It just depends."

Clint nodded. "I understand."

"You should get some rest," Dr. Tyson said, placing a hand on his upper arm. "It could be another long night."

It was.

Clint held her hand, begging her without words to get better. She'd been through so much already. She didn't deserve yet another setback. It was time for her to catch a break.

"I realize you might want to be with your parents," he told her at one point, the room empty of everyone but him. "And I don't blame you, Sam, I truly don't. Lord, when I lost my mom and dad I wished I could have gone with them, but look what happened. I met you." He inhaled sharply. "I've never seen a woman as brave as you. You're amazing, Sam. And you've got the world's biggest heart. I don't think I've ever met anyone who's loved a horse as much as you love Coaster. Coaster needs you, too. Who else on our ranch is going to ride him English? If you die—" He hated that he'd used the word out loud. "If you don't make it," he said, "who's going to remind him that he wasn't born to be a cow pony?"

He bowed his head and prayed, promising to be a better man, and do whatever it was God wanted him to.

They took her away for yet another CAT scan early the next morning. Clint's eyes hurt he needed sleep so badly, but he wouldn't leave. He refused to leave as long as Sam was in a coma.

An hour later, his heart stopped when he saw the doctor approaching. There was a look on the man's face.

"What is it?" he asked. Gigi took his hand. His grandmother had been his anchor for the past forty-eight hours.

"Well," Dr. Tyson said, "I think it's good news."

"Has the swelling gone down?"

"Yes, but more importantly, her embolism is gone."

"Gone?" Gigi asked, clearly as shocked as he was.

Dr. Tyson was nodding. "Gone," he repeated.

"But how?" Gigi asked.

"I can only surmise that the pressure exerted on the brain broke it apart."

Clint couldn't speak for a moment. "You mean it popped?"

"Good Lord, no," Dr. Tyson said. "If that had happened, she'd be dead. No. It's simply gone." He held up his clipboard, pulled out a sheaf of paper from it, drew two lines side-by-side. "An embolism is a blockage. Sometimes it's caused by plaque, sometimes from blood clots. Echo-sonograms indicate that hers was from a blood clot, but there's no way to know for sure without opening her up, which, of course, we can't do. So the blockage was here." He drew a circle on one of the lines. "And as blood passed through her central retinal artery, it collected more dead blood cells." The circle grew bigger. "That's what was causing her to slowly go blind. But now, it's gone, and the only thing that makes sense is that the pressure to her brain somehow broke the clot apart. If it'd become dislodged as a whole, she'd be dead from stroke."

Clint stood there, trying to assimilate it all. Gigi's hand clasped his harder and harder.

"It's a miracle," she said.

"Well," Dr. Tyson said, "that remains to be seen. She might have already suffered permanent damage to her vision. Or not. There's no way to know until she opens her eyes."

And so Clint went back to her room and prepared to wait it out. He didn't care if he had to be there for the rest of his life. Sam would not—she would absolutely not—wake up alone.

Not this time.

IT WAS THE WORLD'S WORST headache. That's what it felt like to Sam. She would lay there, eyes closed, and think to herself, I should probably wake up, maybe go take some aspirin, then the pain would go away. But she could never muster the energy. During one of these conscious moments, she decided she'd had enough. It was time to get up.

She opened her eyes. And became confused. She was *not* in her room. Then she realized she had a tube in her mouth. That sent her into a panic. She tried to cry out, tried to turn her head.

And then Clint leaned over her.

"Sam?"

Where am I? What happened?

She remembered the roundup. Remembered going after that last herd of horses, but beyond that...

"Sam, Can you hear me?"

She tried to tell him with her eyes that she *did*—loud and clear—but he was fading. It was happening then. She was finally losing the vision in her eyes.

SHE WOKE UP WHAT FELT LIKE minutes later, but that Clint would later tell her wasn't for another twenty-four hours. This time the tube was out of her mouth. When she cocked her head and saw Clint sitting in a chair, cowboy hat tipped over his face, feet propped up. She was able to let out a barely audible "Ahem" that came out sounding more like a gag.

He jerked awake.

"Sam."

More gagging.

"It's from the tube," he said, turning and grabbing a cup from somewhere. "They said your throat would feel dry."

They had *that* right, but of course, she'd been through this before.

"Here." He positioned a straw in front of her.

She followed it with her eyes. He held it up to her mouth. "That okay?" he asked.

She nodded, then immediately wished she hadn't. Her head. Dear God, what had she done to her head? Was it related to the embolism?

"Let me call the doctor and tell him you're awake."

"Wha—" Ah, that sounded better. "What." She tried again. "Happened."

"You came off Coaster," he said, holding the cup steady for her.

Her eyes widened.

"Damn horse bucked you off."

"No," she whispered.

He smiled, and then he laughed. "Even as messed up as you are, you still think that damn horse of yours walks on water."

"Does," she said after he helped her take another sip of water.

Clint shook his head, but he was still smiling. "Well, as it happens, you're right. He didn't buck you off, I guess you could say you sort of fell off."

She raised her eyebrows because that was about all she felt like doing.

"Let me call the doctor."

Sam wanted to go back to sleep. She didn't want to

be examined by yet another doctor. Actually, she was pretty certain she did go back to sleep because when she next opened her eyes, a doctor was there.

"Sam, this is Dr. Tyson. He's going to check your vision."

Her vision? What was wrong with her vision? For the first time she realized that something was different.

"Hi, Sam," Dr. Tyson said. He had dark hair and kind blue eyes. "Could you look at my finger, please?"

Sam glanced at Clint before doing as asked.

"Can you see this?" the doctor asked, wiggling a finger back and forth.

She nodded, but slowly this time so it wouldn't hurt.

"Now. Keep your eyes here." He lifted his other hand and Sam suddenly recognized the test she was being given. They were checking her peripheral vision.

"Can you see this hand?" the doctor asked.

Sam just about jerked out of bed. She would have, too, except she knew it would hurt too much…but she could see his hand.

Her eyes must have told the whole story because the doctor smiled. Clint was smiling, too.

"How about the other eye?" the doctor asked. "Can you see this hand, too?" he asked, switching things around.

"Yes," Sam managed to get out. She closed her eyes for a second, hardly daring to believe it. When she opened them again, she could see it all. Her bed, the ceiling above, the window to her right…Clint.

She smiled then, though it felt funny—as if she hadn't used her facial muscles in a long time.

"I can't believe it," Clint said. "I just can't believe it."

"Remarkable," Dr. Tyson admitted.

"What," she gasped out. If she whispered, she

could make herself heard better, she realized. "What did you do to me?"

"They didn't do anything," Clint said, the expression on his face tender. "I think you have a couple of angels in heaven who gave you back your eyes."

Chapter Twenty-Five

She was in the hospital for another week, mostly because her doctors wanted to run a battery of tests. They were mystified and fascinated by her embolism—or lack thereof. There was talk of exciting new research, and maybe even a new technique to treat her condition, all of which Sam listened to with half an ear. She just wanted to get back to the ranch.

And Clint.

He was with her almost every moment of every day, trading places sometimes with Gigi, but there for her in a way Sam had never thought to have. She learned about Lorenzo. He had been found and caught about the time Sam had been lifted out. They hadn't pressed charges—all they could do was go after him for trespassing—but Clint had vowed to do exactly that if the man ever came on his property again, or talked about the mustangs.

When she was released, she went back to the ranch where Gigi promised to take care of her like she'd never been cared for before.

And as the days passed, she had a constant stream of visitors. And so while she still found herself missing her parents—her "angels" in heaven—she was never alone. It was great...

For a while.

The day Sam decided to visit the stable was a day no one on the ranch would ever forget. Clint flat out refused to take her to the barn. He told her she needed to stay off her feet, something that Sam considered ludicrous. She'd been off her feet for weeks, and all she'd had was a really bad concussion. Sure, she still had bouts of dizziness, but she wasn't going to drive a car.

So when Clint wasn't looking (and Gigi was busy in the kitchen) she snuck out. Sunshine warmed her body… and her heart, the smell of springtime wild flowers filling the air. She tipped her head back and simply soaked in the sun. This was what she needed. There was nothing like good old-fashioned UV rays to heal the soul.

"What the *hell* do you think you're doing?"

Uh-oh.

"I *told* you to stay in bed."

She truly hated it when Clint became overprotective. "Clint," she said, meeting his stern expression, "you can't keep me locked away forever. I feel like Rapunzel in there." She pointed to the house behind her. "Except you don't want me to escape the castle. It's ridiculous."

"It's not ridiculous," he said, motioning for her to turn around and march back up the steps she'd been about to sit on.

"No."

"No?" he repeated, crossing his arms in front of him.

"No." She folded her arms, too.

"Don't make me pick you up and carry you."

"Don't make me run."

He lunged, and she darted. But he caught her by the middle. "Clint!" Even though she was furious at his high-handed attitude, she felt a giggle bubble up inside. "Let me go right now."

"Not until I carry you back to bed."

She spun around in his arms, raised an eyebrow and asked, "Do you plan to join me there?"

"No."

She twisted out of his arms, having to work hard to keep the dizziness at bay. "Seriously, Clint, this is getting old. I need to be outside. In the barn, preferably. Someplace other than in the bedroom."

"Not until you get a clean bill of health."

He would brook no argument. And so, frustrated, she went back in the house. Gigi glanced up in surprise from where she stood at the counter, chopping lettuce by the look of it.

"How'd you get outside?"

"I cut through the barbwire," Sam muttered heading upstairs although, technically, she was allowed to recline on the couch.

"Is Clint driving you crazy?" Gigi called after her.

Sam returned reluctantly and dropped into one of the kitchen chairs. "Honestly, Gigi, I don't think I can take much more of this."

"He's got your best interest at heart."

"Yeah, but when's it going to stop?"

Gigi shrugged. Sam stared out the kitchen window. She could see Clint going to the barn. They hadn't been out to gather the last of the mustangs, something they planned to do next week before the weather got too hot and the lower pastures too dry.

"Do you think he loves me?" Sam found herself asking.

Gigi snorted. "If you'd seen him at the hospital that first day when we all thought you might die, you wouldn't have to ask that question."

"No," she said, swiveling on her chair. "Do you think he loves *me*." She tapped her chest. "Not Sam the pitiful soon-to-be-blind woman. Or Sam the head injury victim. But me…Sam the geologist. Sam the champion show-horse rider."

Gigi paused in the middle of what she was doing. "What are you saying?"

She looked out the window again. She was just in time to see Clint disappear into the barn. "It all happened so fast, Gigi. One minute I was asking you about the Baer Mountain Mustangs and the next Clint was holding my hand in the hospital."

Gigi moved toward her, the smell of basil following her. That's what she must've been cutting. "Sometimes things happen that way. You don't need to be afraid it's not real."

Sam looked into Gigi's eyes. "*Is* it real?"

"I don't know," Gigi said. "You tell me."

She couldn't hold the woman's gaze. "I think I need to go away."

"What?"

"Leave…for a little while." Maybe longer than a little while.

"Sam!" Gigi cried. "You can't be serious."

Sam took a deep breath. "I am."

"But—" The woman was at a loss for words.

"Where will I go?" Sam finished for her. "Back to Wilmington. To my apartment. Try to find a job. Repay you for Coaster."

"But that could take months." Gigi sounded truly horrified.

"Maybe not. And maybe the minute I get to Delaware I'll turn around and come back." She felt her stomach churn at the idea of driving away. But what if her feelings for Clint wouldn't stand the test of time? What if this was the equivalent to a cruise ship romance—albeit one with more drama—but a holiday romance nonetheless.

What if?

"Don't be ridiculous," Clint said when she broached the subject with him after lunch. Gigi had left them alone after staring from one to the other as if it might be the last time. "I know what's in my heart."

But, see, that was the problem. *He* knew. I'm right, you're wrong, just do what I say. It drove her nuts. This time, she wasn't going to back down.

"I'm leaving," she said, her heart racing. "Next week."

"Don't be ridiculous," Clint echoed Gigi. He stared at her from across the kitchen table, cowboy hat firmly in place. "You're staying right here."

"Or what?" she asked, tipping her head to the side.

Mistake.

She grew dizzy.

"See," he pounced. "You're feeling light-headed again, I can tell."

"No," she lied. "I'm fine. And the doctors said I'll be okay to drive in a few more days. I'm going back home. Get things settled. Try to figure out where to go from there."

"Your home is here," Clint said.

"Maybe," she admitted.

"Maybe?" But then he shook his head. "Maybe," he repeated, softer this time. "How can you say that after everything we've been through?"

She got up and went to him, touched his arm. They hadn't made love since…well…since before. But as always happened when she caressed his arm she got all fluttery inside. Sexual attraction. They had that in spades.

"It'll just be for a little while," she said gently. "And

I promise to call. I need to do this, Clint. For myself."
And for us. One of them needed to be sensible. It would
be foolish to give up her life in Wilmington, at least not
without testing the waters first.

*That's not what you thought when you were going
blind.*

But she silenced that voice.

"I love you," he said, lifting his hands so he could cup
her face. "I love you more than I ever thought it was
possible to love a woman. Don't do this, Sam. Stay
here. It's where you were meant to be."

"Are you certain?" she asked, holding his gaze with
her own. "Are you absolutely certain?"

"Yes," he said. "What I feel is real. You feel it, too."

Did she? Did she really? Or was it gratitude? Did she
love this man because he'd been kind to her, or because
it was meant to be?

"Don't make this hard on me," she begged.

He moved away.

"Clint, wait. No. Don't let it be like this. It's the right
thing to do. You'll see that once I'm gone."

"Go on then," he said, turning back to her. "If you're
going to leave, you might as well leave now. I'll have
Dean drive you to town. You can stay in a hotel. I'll have
one of the boys follow with your car."

"Clint, no, I don't have to leave now—"

He all but slammed the kitchen door.

"Damn," she muttered. "Damn, damn, damn."

She didn't *want* to leave now. She wanted a chance
to say goodbye to the place. To Gigi. To her *horse.*

"You need help packing?" Gigi asked a few
seconds later.

"I think he kicked me out."

"He's hurt, Sam. Seeing you here. Knowing you're

going to leave. He knows it'll only make him hurt worse. He's just trying to protect himself."

She hadn't thought of it that way. "Then I guess maybe he's right."

"You want Dean to drive you into town?"

She hesitated for a moment, but there was no backing down now. "Yes," she said firmly.

As she headed upstairs, she wrestled with her conscience. *Turn around, go find Clint, tell him you were wrong. But what if I'm not wrong?*

She packed with Gigi's help, and when Dean pulled up in his truck, she prepared to climb inside. Clint stood near one of the barn's double doors, his body erect, his gaze intense even from that distance.

"Did you want to say goodbye to Coaster?" Gigi asked.

Yes. She wanted to see her horse. Desperately. But she didn't think she could bear to see the recriminations in Clint's eyes.

"Give him a kiss on the nose for me, would you?" Sam climbed inside.

"Please don't do this," Gigi implored.

Sam sucked in a deep breath. "I have to, Gigi. It's the right thing to do for *both* of us."

She glanced back at the barn. Clint was still standing there.

Please don't let me leave without saying goodbye.

He spun on his heel and walked away, his body swallowed by the shadow of the barn.

Chapter Twenty-Six

A million times during the next few days Sam told herself to go back. It would have been so easy to get into her car and drive herself to the ranch—or to *have* someone drive her back.

She loved Clint. She was sure she did. Whether or not she loved him for the *right* reasons, though, *that* remained to be seen. Clint needed this break, too. He might not admit that to himself...*yet*...but one day he would thank her.

She called him when she made it safely back to Delaware, but it was Gigi who picked up. She asked to talk to Clint but Gigi told her he was busy, even though Sam could clearly hear him in the background, refusing to take her call.

"Give it time, Sam," Gigi whispered into the phone.

"Tell him..." She struggled to get the words out. "Tell him I love him."

God. Why did saying those words out loud fill her with terror?

"I will," Gigi said gently.

It was a terror that only grew in the succeeding days. Try as she might she couldn't understand why. Why was she afraid of picking up stakes and moving to Montana?

Was it because she didn't want to lose everything she'd worked so hard to create for herself in Wilmington?

Or maybe it was the thought of letting go.

At last she understood.

It was scary to leave everything behind. Her friends, a city she loved…everything. But rather than assuage her fears, figuring out their cause only made her feel worse. How in the hell was this all going to work out? Would Clint let her be true to herself? If she did pick up stakes and move to Montana, would he mind her working off the ranch? Did he expect her to stay home, have children, raise a family?

"He's busy," Gigi said for the umpteenth time when Sam called to ask him exactly that.

"Don't give me that, Gigi," Sam said. "Put him on."

"Sam—"

"Now!"

"All right, all right…"

She heard the muffled sounds of Gigi talking with her hand over the phone, then Clint came on.

"Yeah," he said.

"Stop it."

"Excuse me?"

"You're acting like a baby." Wait. That wasn't what she'd meant to say.

"Excuse me," he said, louder.

"We have important matters to discuss and you're pouting and refusing to pick up the phone."

"I haven't had anything to say to you."

Sam took a deep breath. "What if I don't want kids?"

"We'll breed show horses then," he said instantly.

"What if I want to keep my job?"

"You don't *have* a job."

"Actually, I got my old job back. I start next week."

Silence.

"So, I was thinking—"

She waited for him to say something, anything, that might encourage her. He didn't.

"I was thinking," she began again. "Maybe I could commute to the ranch on weekends."

"Commute," he repeated.

"Yeah. And then, maybe eventually, I could find a job out there."

She waited.

"No."

"Excuse *me?*" she said.

"I said no, Sam."

"Why?"

"Because it's all or nothing. Either you come live with us here on the ranch. *Live.* I'm not talking marriage, not at first if you don't want, just be here with us. Or stay there."

"That's ridiculous."

"Is it?" he asked. "Don't you think it's time to step up to the plate? To make a commitment one way or the other."

"We hardly know each other."

She heard him release a huff of anger. "If you still think that way by now, this isn't going to work out."

"That's not true—"

"Goodbye, Sam."

"Clint, wait—"

He hung up on her. She tried calling him back. The phone rang and rang and rang.

"Impossible man."

She went for a walk. She'd taken to going on long strolls in the park during the afternoon. Every once in a while she'd bump into a mounted patrol. That's what she needed, she thought. The smell of horse to soothe her nerves. But there were no police officers in sight, so she kept walking.

What was wrong with her?

It was times like these that she missed her parents the most. She wished she had a girlfriend, or someone close she could talk to, but she'd always kept to herself. That was part of her problem, she realized. She liked her independence. Suddenly, she was faced with being a part of something—something big—and it scared her to death.

She called Clint the next day, but he flat out refused to get on the phone. Gigi sounded distant, too, and Sam knew the time had come to make a decision. Either she went back to Montana or she stopped calling.

A week later she knew it was hopeless.

She loved Clint. This wasn't some weeklong fling. This was *real*.

So. Go back to him.

But as she looked around the park for what must have been the tenth time in as many days, she shook her head. She didn't think she could do it. She was terrified that if she threw her heart into the ring, committed herself to Clint and to Gigi and to the ranch, she would end up losing herself in the process.

So she started back to work. But it wasn't the same. Point of fact, her job was boring. It was nothing like chasing wild horses. Or sorting cows. Or eating hamburgers by a campfire.

"Damn it," she cursed two weeks later as she was checking core samples. She hadn't talked to Clint. Not once in three weeks.

"What is it?" one of her coworkers asked, a geeky-looking man who Sam was convinced had a crush on her.

"I need to take a break."

"You look like you need one," he said.

She shrugged off her lab coat.

"You going to the park?" he asked.

"Yeah." Everyone knew her routine. She came back smelling like a horse half the time.

Two minutes later she was walking out of the building. She worked in downtown Wilmington, a city that housed some of the nation's largest chemical companies. Her employer, Dell Chemical, was housed in one of the many high-rises that dotted downtown and she was immediately plunged into the shadows those buildings created.

She needed sunshine.

The panic she'd been feeling more and more of late was back. The same anxiety she'd felt when she realized she was in love with Clint. But it'd been weeks since they'd last talked. He was mad at her, maybe even to the point that he didn't want to see her again. She wouldn't blame him if he did. It was her fault. She should have been braver. Followed her heart. They could have sorted everything out when she got back to Montana. Instead she'd taken the easy way out. A comfortable routine over the unknown.

A job over Clint.

"Idiot," she said, sitting on a park bench. She wiped her face. Somewhere between Eighth and Ninth Streets she'd started to cry.

Just go to him, Sam.

But she was afraid, she thought, clutching her head. She was terrified. Barely able to breathe, hands shaking terrified.

Of losing Clint.

Her head popped up.

Of losing someone she loved. Again.

"Oh, crap," she said, wiping her eyes. "Crap, crap, crap."

She loved Clint. She loved Gigi, too. She loved the ranch. But she'd detached herself from them. Not because she wanted to keep her life in Wilmington—no. Because she couldn't face the thought of losing someone again.

Like she'd lost her parents.

"Oh, Mom," she muttered. "I'm such an idiot."

She heard horses hooves and straightened up. She needed to hug a horse right now, needed to inhale that horse's scent that always soothed her nerves. She'd have to quit her job. Give notice on her apartment, too.

That's when she saw him. It was Clint.

Clint rode toward her.

She thought she was seeing things at first, couldn't quite accept that there was a cowboy—not a police officer—riding in the park. And he led a horse, too. He led Coaster.

She started to cry.

It was a miracle.

"Lady," he said, pulling Buttercup up in front of her, "I thought I'd have to ride around this park all damn day."

"How did you find me?" she asked, quickly wiping her eyes again as she stood up.

"It was an inside job," Clint said. Buttercup tried sniffing her, but Sam went straight to Coaster, placing her forehead in between her horse's eyes and trying—really, truly trying—not to cry even harder. "I called your boss, told him what I planned to do. He told me you liked to walk in the park."

"I do," she said. "I like to pet the mounted patrol's horses."

"You don't need to do that," he said, slipping off.

She felt her shoulders flex as she held back a sob.

"Your own horse is right here," he said, stopping in

front of her, nudging her around and into his arms. "And so am I."

"Oh, Clint," she said. "I've been such an idiot."

"Shh," he soothed, somehow managing to hold her and the horses' reins at the same time. "You're not an idiot."

"I was scared of losing you. Afraid you might end up dying on me, too. I didn't realize it at first, but that's why I left you and Gigi and even Coaster here." She reached out and stroked his nose.

"I'm not going to die on you."

"I know. I mean, what would be the odds of that? But I'm still so afraid."

"Don't be," he said, holding her close.

"I didn't want to hurt anymore. I miss my parents so damn much."

"I know you do. But you have *me* now," he said gently.

"I realize that," she murmured. "I really do, but the truth is, it hurts even *more* to be away from you. At least when I'm with you I don't feel that horrible ache. And I know why, too. It's because I feel as if I'm missing a part of myself."

"Sam," he said, tipping her head back and kissing her.

She kissed him back, tried to show him without words how sorry she was. She'd missed the taste of him, missed the way his kisses made her feel: Wanted. Needed. *Loved.*

"I love you," she whispered a long while later. "I love you more than I ever thought it was possible to love someone. I'll move to Montana. Tomorrow if you want me to. And I'll let you turn Coaster into a cow pony. I'll even learn how to cook over a campfire."

"That horse will never be a pony," he said.

She started laughing. He did, too, and when she looked past him, she saw Gigi near the edge of the riding path, a wide grin spread across her face.

"I'm thinking a wedding at the ranch," Gigi said, reaching out and patting Coaster's side as she walked past. "In December, the month of miracles, 'cause it sure is a miracle the two of you finally, *thankfully* came to your senses."

"Oh, Gigi." Sam wiped her eyes yet again.

"Now you two get on and ride. I wanted to take pictures. Need to show them to my future great-grandchildren."

And years later, that's exactly what she did.